Puffin Plus

MURPHY & CO

'Just wait till I get my feet back under the boardroom table,' said Charlie Russell. 'Then I'll sort them all out – including high and mighty Mac Murphy.'

With new players, an improved ground and the promise of half a million pounds in the coffers, it seems that Dunmore United has every chance of promotion. But Mac's hopes are dashed when Rasputin refuses the money. What's behind the refusal, and how will the club manage?

While jealousy and intrigue absorb those in high places, Murphy's Mob are struggling with their own problems. Is Sheila ditching Gerry for the club's star player? Is Mac's younger brother being blackmailed? And what's a nice girl like Becky Marsh doing with the odious Bernie Russell?

Another great read for fans of *Murphy's Mob*, with much more than just football!

MURPHY & CO.

by Anthony Masters
adapted from the Central Television series
by Brian Finch

PUFFIN BOOKS

Puffin Books, Penguin Books Ltd, Harmondsworth, Middlesex, England
Penguin Books, 625 Madison Avenue, New York, New York 10022, U.S.A.
Penguin Books Australia Ltd, Ringwood, Victoria, Australia
Penguin Books Canada Ltd, 2801 John Street, Markham, Ontario, Canada L3R 14
Penguin Books (N.Z.) Ltd, 182–190 Wairau Road, Auckland 10, New Zealand

First published 1983

Set in Linotron Plantin by
Rowland Phototypesetting Ltd
Bury St Edmunds, Suffolk
Made and printed in Great Britain by
Cox and Wyman Ltd, Reading

1

The gym was very modern, high and wide, a bit like a brightly painted miniature aircraft hangar. In the centre of the echoing space was a boxing ring and surrounding it was a circle of shouting, excited schoolkids. The two boys in the ring had been sparring for some time when they suddenly ran into each other with a flurry of punches – and their audience went wild with cheers and shouts. Almost immediately the burly figure of Mr Briggs stepped in to separate them and the two boys broke. They had a good deal of respect for their Sports Master who managed to combine no-nonsense aggression with kindness and humour.

One of the combatants, Boxer, a skilful fifteen-year-old, was now very much on top, driving his opponent back into the corner of the ring and causing him to cover his face with his gloves. The audience roared again and the bell went for the end of the P.E. period.

'All right,' said Mr Briggs. 'That's enough.' The two boys touched gloves and grinned good-naturedly at each other. 'Saved by the bell, eh?' laughed Mr Briggs to Jordan who had just been pulverized by Boxer. Jordan gave him a rueful look and then Mr Briggs turned to the class. 'All right – go and get changed, you lot.' His broad Yorkshire accent gave the brusqueness of his tone a kindly note. As Boxer followed his class-mates out, Mr Briggs stopped him and said, 'Not you, Reed – I want a word wi' you.' Boxer looked up at him, wondering what he had done wrong.

'There's a town team match a week Friday night and one

of their best lads has dropped out – which lets you in. Right?'

Boxer was delighted. 'Yes, sir. That'll be great.'

Mr Briggs gave him a friendly scowl.

'Right then. Go and get changed – and be quick about it. And put those gloves away.'

As Boxer ran to do as he was told his spirits rose. Life was great!

Some of the members of the Junior Supporters' Club of Dunmore United were having a kick-around outside the rather scruffy gates of the ground when the Rolls Royce glided into view. It looked out of place in the shabby street, its gleaming coachwork and highly polished chrome a marked contrast to the peeling paintwork of the houses and the other battered cars parked by the side of the road.

Behind the wheel of the Rolls was Charlie Russell, a flash bookie who had originally been Chairman of Dunmore United. Since his replacement by Rasputin Jones he had been trying to cause trouble for the club. Beside him was one of his friends – a rather sinister man called Ivor Chalmers. His face hardly ever expressed anything but cold disinterest and his eyes were dead. He looked at the kids booting the ball around with tepid disapproval and then, turning to Russell, said, 'Who's that lot?'

'Scruffs,' returned Charlie Russell decisively. 'They come from this crummy housing estate and they've terrorized this ground for years.'

'Can't the manager get rid of them?' Chalmers intoned in his lifeless voice.

'Get rid of them?' Charlie Russell laughed angrily. 'The manager flaming well encourages them.'

'What for?' asked Chalmers bleakly.

'Listen,' said Charlie. 'And I'll tell you a story. When Big Mac Murphy took this place over last year, he never even tried to get rid of them. Not Mac. The flaming idiot actually

6

suggested they even formed their own Junior Supporters' Club and gave them a club-room in the ground.'

'Good grief,' said Chalmers and for the first time his face betrayed scornful emotion.

'Yeah,' said Charlie with feeling. 'So the ground's become a focal point for every yobbo in the area.'

As if to underline this, the ball suddenly bounced high in the air and landed on the highly polished roof of the Rolls.

'Blimey,' said Charlie. 'That does it.'

'That's done it,' said Wurzel.

'Bet you've dented it,' replied the Prof, polishing his glasses and looking as if he were about to take on an avenging army.

Gonk grinned, his black face wreathed in a doom-laden grin. 'You've done it now, man. When you gonna learn to control the ball?'

'Shut your mouth,' said Wurzel as he strode unhappily towards the Rolls. Already he could see an infuriated Charlie Russell emerging from it, shaking his fist at them.

'Send the bill to your dad,' shouted Fozzy Berford, but his voice held a tremor of fear. All four kids could see how enraged Charlie Russell was.

'Sorry,' said Wurzel as he ran up to the Rolls to collect the ball.

'Sorry?' snarled Russell. 'You'll be sorry if you've damaged my coachwork.'

Furiously he inspected the roof of the Rolls and then seemed almost disappointed when he could see no damage. He then turned on Wurzel while the other three stood a few yards away, uneasily staring at their feet.

'Don't you know the laws about playing football in the street?'

'But this isn't the street,' returned the Prof from his safe distance. 'It's the forecourt of the club.'

'Don't give me any of your lip,' snapped Charlie, walking a few paces toward him.

'Can we have our ball back, mister?' asked Wurzel meekly, indicating that it had come to rest just behind the Rolls.

Chalmers looked at him as if he were Oliver Twist asking for more, while all Charlie could say was: 'Well – of all the flippin' nerve.' Then he stalked behind the Rolls and picked up the football.

'It's confiscated,' he said, opening the boot and hurling it contemptuously inside. Smiling for the first time, Chalmers got out of the Rolls and stood by his side. Charlie locked the car and ignoring the kids, said to Chalmers, 'Come on – I'll show you round.'

'Please, sir,' began Wurzel ingratiatingly. 'The ball ain't ours.'

'Bad luck,' returned Charlie, and Chalmers continued to grin as if this was the first joke he had appreciated in years. Both of them strode through the open gate of the ground and all four kids watched their departure with dismay. Then Gerry and Boxer joined them. Both were bigger than the other four and had an air of leadership and authority to them.

'So who's been shouting the odds?' asked Gerry, and Gonk replied miserably, 'Charlie Russell.'

'The bookie?' asked Boxer.

'That's him.'

'I thought Rasputin had kicked him off the board last season.'

'He did,' said Wurzel. 'But that didn't stop him nicking our ball.'

'What he means,' said Gonk, 'is that the ball belongs to Mac.'

'So it's rather an interesting situation,' explained the Prof.

'Then there's only one thing to do,' said Boxer, 'and that's to see Mac right away.'

They ran through the gates of Dunmore United, leaving behind them the gleaming Rolls with the ball firmly locked in its gleaming boot.

Mac Murphy sat at his desk in his small office under Dunmore United's main stand. He hated paperwork but nevertheless he knew it was an essential part of the job he enjoyed. Despite his impulsive and often irritating Chairman, Rasputin Jones, Mac had settled into his job and was now determined to begin to work the run-down old club up the League. He knew that Rasputin had a sneaking trust in him now – and he also suspected that the aggressive, thirty-year-old ex-pop-singer had a sneaking respect for him too. Elaine, Mac's much loved wife, adviser and part-time secretary, was putting her coat on before going home and cooking him his tea.

'Will you be long?' she asked.

''Bout half an hour,' he grunted.

'Well,' Elaine replied briskly. 'Make sure it's no longer or your bangers will be burnt to a frazzle.'

As she opened the door she almost collided with Wurzel, Gonk, Boxer and Gerry. They all looked guilty and apprehensive.

'The Mafia are here,' she announced.

'We'd like a word with Mac,' said Wurzel.

'Thought you might,' said Elaine, as she went out. 'Don't keep him from his tea then.'

Mac looked up as the kids trooped in. He was secretly proud of the Junior Supporters' Club and the way he had taken them off the streets to a more positive interest. But he always treated them firmly and he knew he was right – for they often presented him with problems.

'Well, what's the bad news?' he asked.

'You know that ball we borrowed,' Wurzel began hesitantly.

'Which ball?'

'Well – we *would* have asked you if we could borrow it – if you'd been here.' Wurzel's wheedling tone was very uneasy.

'Where was it?' Mac's voice was hollow.

'In the players' room. It was just lying around and –'

'You mean a match ball, do you?' Mac's temper began to rise.

'Well – maybe – yes.'

'So – where is it? You haven't lost it, have you? They cost a bomb.'

'Not exactly lost it,' said Wurzel miserably.

'What do you mean – not exactly lost it?'

'It's been nicked,' said Boxer woodenly.

Charlie Russell and Ivor Chalmers were looking up at the seating on the stand.

'Well,' said Chalmers reluctantly. 'You've got to hand it to Rasputin. He's certainly tarted the place up since he took over as Chairman.'

But Charlie was quick to disagree. 'He spent it the wrong way. He should have put it into better players – not better seating.'

Just then Ted, the untidy old groundsman, came up behind them.

'Oi!'

They turned to find him glaring at them.

'Are you speaking to us?' said Ivor Chalmers in icy tones.

'Well – I'm not speaking to a flaming lamp-post, am I?'

Charlie Russell laughed mirthlessly. 'Ivor – this is Ted – a real club character. Good to see you, Ted.'

But Ted had no intention of being friendly. 'Wish I could say the same, Mr Russell. But I reckon it would choke me.'

'So what's the problem?' asked Charlie, in a harder voice.

'You've got your feet on my playing surface.'

'We're doing no harm.'

'As official groundsman,' began Ted, 'I'll be the judge of that. I'll trouble you to move.'

Reluctantly they complied and Ted grinned. He loved scoring points off his old enemy and this had been an ideal opportunity.

'Stupid old nit,' observed Charlie as he and Chalmers walked slowly away. 'I can tell you, if I'd had my way he'd have been kicked out years ago.'

Ted, meanwhile, strode towards the tunnel, where he met Mac and the kids.

'You've got visitors. Unwelcome ones.'

'So I hear.' Mac strode on until he reached Charlie Russell and Ivor Chalmers who were walking slowly towards the gate.

'Looking for me, gentlemen?' he asked brusquely.

'Not particularly,' returned Charlie coldly.

'Oh, I thought you might have been looking for me. Seeing as I'm the manager.'

'I was showing Mr Chalmers round. That's all.'

'Oh, aye? Why don't you ask next time? In fact – try asking me.'

'Friendly soul, aren't you?' said Charlie acidly.

'And before you go – that ball you took off the kids. It's a match ball and club property so I'd be grateful if you'd return it.'

Speechlessly, Charlie and Ivor walked away and Mac knew that he had won. He glanced back to where the boys were standing grinning at the tunnel entrance.

'And don't let me find you borrowing match balls without permission. Eh?'

'No, Mac,' said Wurzel ruefully. 'We won't.'

*

'And who's Charlie Russell when he's at home?'

Wurzel, Fozzy and the Prof were standing round the pool table. Fozzy, who was an excellent pool player, was giving Wurzel a thrashing and he asked the question as he made a break.

'He's a bookie,' replied Wurzel, 'and he's as bent as a three quid note.'

'Is he Bernie Russell's dad?'

'That's 'im. Now there's another tasty boy for yer. Know what he did last year? Only smashed up the Senior Supporters' Club – that's all. *And* he tried to blame it on Boxer.'

'Why should he do that?' asked Fozzy, lining up his next shot.

'Boxer didn't want him in the Club – so he tried to get Boxer into trouble.'

'What happened?'

'Big Mac sorted it out,' said the Prof. 'And Bernie got slung out of the Club and his dad off the board. Which makes you wonder.'

'Wonder what?' asked Fozzy, lining up another shot.

'If Charlie Russell's back – what's he up to this time?' said the Professor, taking his glasses off and wiping them. The other two looked up at him in alarm.

Boxer was living with Big Mac and Elaine while his parents were abroad. He loved being with them and it also gave him the opportunity to keep up his almost fanatical interest in Dunmore United. For their part, Mac and Elaine had grown equally fond of the boy and there was a sense of peace as Elaine cleared away their tea of bangers and mash. But that sense of peace was broken immediately when Big Mac took up the very subject that had been worrying Fozzy, Wurzel and the Prof.

'Well, I'll tell you this, love,' said Mac to Elaine's back. 'It bodes no good for us with Charlie Russell prowling around.' Then he looked across at Boxer, noticing that he had a fat lip. 'How did you get that?'

'A kid got a left hook through my guard.'

'You've not been fighting, have you, Boxer?' asked Elaine anxiously.

''Fraid so.'

'Oh, no.'

Boxer grinned at her. 'I was doing school boxing training.'

Elaine returned his grin but still looked anxious. She hated boxing and was sure that Boxer would get hurt one day – badly hurt.

'I've got some news for you,' said Boxer a little warily, for he knew Elaine's views – and in some ways respected them. 'I've been picked to fight for the town team a week on Friday night.'

'Short-handed, were they?' asked Mac, stirring his tea.

'Something like that.'

'Congrats.'

'Ta.'

But Elaine needed to say her piece. 'Why is it that the only sports that interest men involve violence? Can't you ever play any gentle games?'

'I can just see young Boxer playing netball,' grunted Mac.

'For your information, Mac Murphy, there are few more vicious games than netball – and I speak from deep, personal experience.'

Mac laughed. 'And you have a go at us for violence. Why don't you tell Boxer about that time you got banned for cleaning out the shooter in that cup final.'

'Get lost.' Elaine hurried out into the kitchen, determined not to be drawn.

Boxer turned to Mac. 'Are you going to come and watch me Friday night then?'

Mac grinned at him. 'Friday night's a busy night for me – we'll see.'

But Boxer was satisfied, for he knew that Mac would come if he possibly could.

'Have you written to your mum and dad yet?'

'Not yet.'

'Then do so.'

'Yes, Boss.'

The next day, old Ted the groundsman was having problems starting his ancient and temperamental motor mower. Cursing, he bent over it, pulling morosely at this lever and the other. He was being watched with deep interest by Wurzel and the Prof.

'Having problems, Ted?' asked Wurzel, stating the obvious.

Glaring at him, Ted replied, 'No – I always spend half a day pressing the starter button. Keeps me fingers slim.'

'I must tell my sister about that, Ted,' replied Wurzel. 'She's a right slimming nut.'

'It's Mr Bridges to you, son.'

Ted started fiddling with his machine again and the Prof said, 'Reckon it's flooded myself.'

'Expert, are you?'

'A bit. Me mum always floods ours.'

'I'm not your mum. Keep your nose out of it, son.'

'I was just trying to help.'

'The best way you lot can help me is to organize a sit-in on the fast lane of a motorway.' He returned to struggle with his mower.

'Could be the battery,' said Wurzel.

Red in the face, Ted looked up and gave vent to a wild cry of rage. The Prof and Wurzel beat a hasty retreat, and Ted gave the mower an almighty kick.

From the doorway, Wurzel shouted, 'That's what you call a kick start, isn't it, Ted?'

'I'd like a word,' said Ted.

Mac was en route to Rasputin in the hope that he would buy in Joey Collins who was on the Transfer List for twenty grand. He said impatiently, 'Not now, Ted. I'm busy. Can it wait?'

'It can wait seasons.'

'What do you mean?'

'I mean it depends on whether you want the pitch mowed for the first match next week.'

'What's the problem –'

'The mower's up the spout.'

'Can't you fix it?'

'It's clapped out. Finito.'

'Look – I'm just off to see the Chairman. I'll bring it to his attention.'

'Do that – and if you don't, I'll resign.'

'Ted –'

'I mean it – I've had enough of the old soft soap.'

And with that he strode off. Mac sighed. Ted had a point.

Becky Marsh didn't want to go into the tatty club-house of
the Junior Supporters' Club but there didn't seem much
choice. The pressures on her were too intense. Reluctantly
she looked at the poster advertising the disco – and then
walked slowly inside. Becky was an attractive thirteen-year-
old and she had every reason to be confident about her
appearance. It was just that she wasn't very confident about
her purpose.

When Becky got inside she found Sheila and Jenny
sorting out drinks at the bar, while Boxer and Gerry were
stacking records and tinkering with the record player.
Becky went straight over to Boxer and said, 'Excuse me.'

'Why – what have you done?' was the laconic reply.

But she didn't laugh, merely contenting herself with a
cold look.

'Can I get tickets here for tonight's disco?'

'S'right.'

'I'd like two.'

'Fine – but give us a minute, love. I'm up to my neck.
Know what I mean?'

'I'm in a hurry.'

'So am I.' Boxer was annoyed that she didn't respond to
him and had remained so cold. With slow deliberation he
turned to Gerry. 'Try it now.'

Gerry put on a record and pop music boomed out.

'That's great,' said Gerry.

'O.K.' Boxer turned back to Becky. 'How many was it?'

'Two, please.' She was still distant, still haughty. Boxer went over to get the tickets which were near the cash box. 'That'll be a quid. Sorry I can't give it to you cheaper.' He gave her a cocky grin.

'You Boxer Reed?'

'That's me.'

'Yes – I thought you were.'

Disdainfully she walked out of the club-house. Gerry came up to Boxer's side with a big grin on his face.

'Who would that be?'

'Never saw her in me life.'

'She knows you – doesn't she?'

'Looks like it. I wonder how?'

Becky Marsh joined Bernie Russell on the forecourt of the club. He was sitting on his bike and holding hers.

'Got 'em?'

Becky took her bike from him.

'I got 'em. That's a quid you owe me.'

'Cheap at twice the price.' He handed her the money and she stared at him, puzzled and suspicious.

'Why did I have to go for them? Why couldn't you?'

'Got me reasons. Anyway – you're a liberated female, aren't you?'

He gave her an unpleasant leer and pedalled off. Slowly she followed him.

Derek Cassidy, secretary of the Senior Supporters' Club, was in Rasputin's office, handing him a cheque.

'There we are, Mr Jones. The proceeds from our Annual Supporters' Club dance. That's another cheque towards the Club development fund.'

'Thanks, Derek – that's most welcome.'

'We like to do our little bit,' Derek replied smugly.

'How would we manage without you?' Rasputin grinned a little sarcastically, for he had never liked the man.

'I see the Juniors are having a disco tonight.'

'Oh, yes.'

Derek smiled in an oily way. 'Let's keep our fingers crossed that there won't be any trouble.'

'There'd better not be.'

Derek Cassidy hesitated. 'I suppose their proceeds go into their own funds.'

'I'm afraid everyone's not got your warm and generous nature, Derek,' said Rasputin blandly.

Cassidy smiled and said, 'I'd best be off. Someone has to prepare the agenda for tonight's A.G.M.'

There was a knock at the door and Derek Cassidy opened it to find Wurzel, the Prof and Fozzy on the threshold.

'Well – what do you lot want?' Cassidy ill concealed his loathing of the kids.

'We want to go roller-skating.'

'Well you can't – the rink's closed,' returned Cassidy.

'Why?' asked Wurzel.

'Because I own it – and because I say so,' said Rasputin from behind his desk. 'Now – why don't you buzz off?'

But just as the kids turned away to leave, Big Mac Murphy arrived. Cassidy, anxious to know what Mac wanted, decided to hang around as Mac threw himself into a chair. Rasputin frowned, for he could sense the purpose in Mac and knew he was going to have some kind of battle on his hands. Gloomily, he knew that it must be about money – the subject that they continually battled over.

'So what's going on?' asked Mac. 'I thought Saturday was your busiest day at the rink.'

'It used to be,' said Rasputin gloomily.

'So – closed for redecorating, are you?'

'Closed for good.'

'How come?'

'Kids can't afford three quid any more – or their parents can't.'

'So what happens to the place now?'

'I'm thinking of opening it as a Chapel of Rest. Now, what's your problem?'

'Joey Collins. He's available.'

'I read that.'

'He's one of the best mid-field men in the game.'

'Agreed.'

'At twenty grand he's a steal.'

'Agreed. So steal him.'

'It's all a –'

'But don't come to me for twenty grand.'

Mac stared at him in open disbelief.

'Because I ain't got it.'

'Since when?'

'Since kids stopped going roller-skating and going to football matches. I tell you – we could soon be in the business of selling players, not buying them.'

'It's as bad as that?'

'Worse.'

'In that case, there's not much point in mentioning the other thing.'

'What other thing?'

'Old Ted needs a new mower.'

'What's wrong with the one he's got?'

'Won't start.'

'Tell 'im to buy a new battery. Right?'

'Right.'

Mac wearily got up and walked out. Once he had gone Derek Cassidy turned to Rasputin and said very sweetly, 'It's extraordinary, Mr Chairman, isn't it?'

Rasputin looked up at him suspiciously. 'Extraordinary – what do you mean?'

'How some people think money grows on trees.'

Mac looked at Boxer unbelievingly as he combed his hair in front of the mirror. He then turned to Elaine, who was reading the paper.

'If I hadn't seen it with my own eyes, I wouldn't have believed it.'

'What?'

'He's combing his hair. In fact from where I'm standing I'd even say he'd had a wash. Or is it the light in here?'

'Ho, ho, ho,' said Boxer.

'Don't tell me some poor misguided female's finally agreed to go out wi' you.'

'Give over, Mac,' returned Boxer. 'Can't dedicate myself to one girl. Wouldn't be fair to the rest of 'em, would it? I'll see you.'

'Don't be late,' said Elaine.

'Back before dawn. Rely on it.'

Boxer went out and Elaine smiled up at Mac. Then she rose and picked up a letter from the mantelpiece.

'He wrote to his mum and dad then.'

'Had to twist his arm.'

'It's worked out all right, hasn't it? Taking him in while they were abroad.'

'You're a mother hen.'

Elaine put her tongue out at him.

'What's the big occasion tonight?' asked Mac.

'Don't you know what goes on at your own club?'

'What do you mean?'

Elaine gave him a fond but impatient glance. 'They're having a disco tonight at the Junior Supporters' Club.'

'What a terrible way to spend an evening.'

'You used to enjoy dancing – in the good old days of the foxtrot and the palais glide.'

'No – I had my speciality. I used to win prizes for it.'

'What was that?'

'The Gay Gordons. What else?' He leant forward and kissed her. Then Elaine said, 'What's worrying you?'

'Nothing.'

'Come on –'

Reluctantly, he told her about Rasputin's financial problems and she said, 'Will it affect the club?'

'I don't know – but –'

'But what?'

'We seem to be getting nowhere,' said Big Mac miserably. 'We're just marking time.'

The disco was in full swing and everyone was enjoying themselves. The club-house was crowded with dozens of kids, all of whom were dancing or drinking coke. Wurzel was acting as a noisy D.J., Gerry and Boxer were guarding the door, and the Prof was selling tickets for a football draw.

After half an hour or so of frantic dancing, Bernie Russell arrived with Becky Marsh – only to receive a hostile welcome from Boxer and Gerry.

'What the hell do you want, Russell?' asked Boxer aggressively.

'Slumming, aren't I? What else?'

'Feel free not to,' said Gerry. 'The way out's right behind you.'

'We've got tickets,' said Becky defensively. 'You sold them to me yourself. Remember?'

'That was before I knew what you was dragging in with you,' replied Boxer.

But Becky was not to be beaten so easily. 'We've every right to come in. Are you saying we can't?'

It was Gerry who decided to give in first. 'Come on, Boxer – let 'em in. Just think of the pleasure we'll have throwing 'im out again if he causes any trouble.'

'All right,' said Boxer. 'Get in.' He turned to Becky. 'Anything for you, love.'

But she was not to be chatted up. 'Thanks for nothing,' she said pertly, stepping inside with Bernie.

'You're welcome,' said Boxer but he looked suddenly angry. Once Bernie and Becky were inside, Boxer said,

'Now what the 'ell's a nice lookin' girl like her doin' with a creep like Bernie?'

'Perhaps you should ask her a bit later on,' said Gerry, stirring it up. 'Give old Bernie a bit of competition.'

Boxer winked at him. 'Maybe I will at that. You never know your luck – p'rhaps he'll start a fight or something – and have to be ejected like.'

Boxer and Gerry began to laugh – they liked the idea of that.

While the disco thrashed on, Mac and Elaine were sitting at home watching television. On the screen flickered the sequinned dresses and black tie and tails of ballroom dancers. The music was smooth, restrained and very strict tempo. Mac was just dozing off when the doorbell rang. Elaine got up to answer it – and returned with Teddy Banks, the reporter from Radio Fairborough. Slumped in his chair, Mac tried to gather himself together.

'Hi, Mac,' said Teddy.

'Got no home to go to, have you?'

'I've got this late night sports spot now – so I thought I'd drop in on my way to the studio.'

'You did, did you?'

'Just for a brief chat.'

'Sit down.'

'Do you want some coffee?' asked Elaine, but Teddy was anxious to come straight to the point.

'No thanks, Mrs Murphy.'

'Well,' said Mac, with greater affability. 'What can I do for you?'

'I just want you to confirm or deny something.'

'What?'

'There's a heavy buzz in town that United's in financial trouble.'

'Is that news? Half the clubs in the First Division are in financial trouble.'

'There's also a story going round that a group of local businessmen are getting together to bail you out.'

'If that means somebody's going to give you some more money to strengthen the playing staff that can only be good news for me. But it's the first I've heard about it.'

But Teddy was becoming tired of Mac's evasiveness and inside himself, Mac was feeling the first waves of panic. What the hell had Teddy picked up? And who were these 'local businessmen'? Teddy homed in, anxious for more positive information.

'So you can't either confirm or deny the buzz?'

'You know more than I do about it. If you hear any more – let me know.'

'I'll do that,' said Teddy with a sigh. 'Thanks, Mac.'

'Thank *you*.'

Mac went thoughtfully to the door with Teddy. When he came back he said to Elaine, 'How about that then?'

'I think it might just explain something.'

'What?'

'It might explain why Charlie Russell was at the ground this afternoon.'

Half-way through the disco, Boxer found Becky standing alone by the tea bar.

'Hi.'

'Hallo.' She was still very off-hand, but Boxer was determined to persevere. He felt oddly attracted to her and was determined to break down her resistance.

'What's your name then?'

'Why do you want to know?'

'You obviously know mine – from what you were saying this morning. Bernie told you, I s'pose.'

'I heard a lot about you from Bernie.'

'Not to the good, eh?'

She gave him a cold look but before he could push her further, Bernie rolled up.

'You want something then?' he asked.

'Just a dance,' returned Boxer.

'Sorry. You're not my type,' Bernie grinned unpleasantly.

'You're a right comic,' said Boxer. 'You'll pardon me if I don't die laughing.' He turned to Becky. 'Well – what do you say?'

'No thanks. I'm with Bernie.'

'That's your bad luck.'

She looked at Boxer angrily and before she could reply, Bernie led her away, back to the gyrating dancers on the floor. As Boxer stared after them, Gonk joined him and said helpfully, 'Well – you've either got it or you haven't, eh?'

'Yeah – we all know what Bernie Russell's got besides bad breath.'

'Bread, man, bread.'

Boxer paused reflectively as he watched Bernie and Becky dancing together. 'Funny though. I wouldn't have thought that sort of thing would 'ave impressed a kid like her.'

Mac was watching Match of the Day when the doorbell rang again and he groaned. Then Elaine came in with Rasputin Jones. Mac rose to switch the television off but Rasputin said, 'Don't turn it off. I can only stay a minute.'

Mac turned to stare at him quizzically while Rasputin said, 'Guess who I got a call from this evening?'

'Teddy Banks of Radio Fairborough?'

'Besides him.'

'Who?'

'Your old friend and mine – Charlie Russell.'

'He was down the ground this afternoon.'

'So he said.'

'What else?'

'He's learned about our little financial problem, and he'd like to introduce us to a friend of his who might help.'

'No friend of Charlie Russell's can be a friend of ours,' said Mac firmly.

'Yeah – that was *my* first reaction.'

'And your second?'

'I invited him to come and see me. After all – there's no charge for listening, is there, Mac?'

Mac was silent for a moment. Then he said, 'In this case – I've got an idea there might be.'

Sheila and Jenny were at the tea bar when Becky came up to them.

'Can I ask you something?'

'Course,' said Sheila.

'How do you join the Junior Supporters' Club?'

'You just join.'

'What forms do you have to fill in?'

'I'll get you one.'

'I'd like two, please.'

Jenny looked at Becky thoughtfully while Sheila paused.

'The other one wouldn't be for Bernie Russell, would it?'

'So?'

'You'll be wasting your time, love. Or Bernie will.'

'Why?' asked Becky.

'All new members have to be voted on by the committee,' said Jenny. 'And Bernie wouldn't get a vote. Not one.'

'Why have you lot all got your knife into Bernie?' Becky burst out angrily.

'You'd better ask him,' said Sheila.

'I'd still like two, please.'

Sheila calmly handed her the two forms without saying anything.

'Thanks,' said Becky. She turned to look for Bernie and then paused.

The music had become very heavy now and a number of boys were dancing by themselves in the middle of the floor. Everyone's eyes were on them and they were involved in some violent head banging. The most prominent of these was Bernie Russell. At that moment Gerry and Boxer came in from their position at the door and spotted him.

'Right,' said Boxer. 'That's it then.' He hurried over to where Wurzel was gyrating madly over the turntable and shouted, 'Take it off.'

'What? It's my favourite track, is this.'

'I said – take it off.'

'All right.'

Wurzel reluctantly took the record off and the music came to a dead stop. Then Boxer marched over to Bernie.

'Knock it off,' he said.

'Eh?'

'I said knock off the head banging.'

'I can dance the way I want to,' said Bernie indignantly, and there was an expectant hush from the boys around him. They smelt trouble – and they could see trouble.

'Not in here you can't. Can't you read?'

'Course I can read.'

'Then look at the notice on the wall. It says "No head banging allowed in discos". So either knock it off or get out.'

As Becky came to join him, Bernie tried to look as if he was going to square up to Boxer. Boxer moved forward in anticipation and the crowd slowly began to form a circle.

Then Becky said, 'Come on, Bernie. It's not worth it.'

Bernie glared up at Boxer and the crowd looked disappointed. As Bernie walked off the floor with Becky, he said loudly, 'I'll fix him one day. I'll really fix him.'

'Any time,' said Boxer, but Bernie was already through the doors. Once outside he turned to Becky furtively and said, 'Did you get the membership forms?'

'What's the point?'

'*Did* you get 'em?'

'I got them. But I want to know what the point is?'

'What do you mean?'

'There's no point in joining if they don't want you in. I mean – if you *did* get in they'd only give you a bad time.'

'I'll tell you this. If anybody's going to get a bad time it's them not me.'

'I don't understand.'

'You will, love. You will. Before Boxer and his mates are very much older – they're in for the shock of their sweet lives.'

'I wouldn't have believed I'd ever see the day.'

Boxer was lacing up his shoes the next morning as Mac and Elaine talked in the living room.

'What day?' asked Mac, who was preparing to go out.

'When I'd hear Rasputin crying poverty.'

'I wouldn't say he was crying poverty – I'd say he was just feeling the draught like everyone else in this country.' He turned briskly to Boxer. 'Do you want a lift to the club?'

'Yes, please.'

'Right, let's go. I'll call you later.'

''Bye, love,' said Elaine.

'Shouldn't you be at school?' asked Mac, as he and Boxer hurried down the stairs.

'We don't go back yet. We're on holiday for another three weeks.'

'I missed my real vocation,' said Mac. 'I should have been a schoolteacher.'

'Well, if you were,' said Boxer, 'at least you'd know when the holidays were.'

Mac aimed a friendly punch at him but Boxer dodged and ran on down the stairs ahead of him.

Becky had called at Bernie Russell's home and now they were standing together in the living-room. Becky discerned a slightly conspiratorial atmosphere and she felt vaguely uneasy.

'Filled your form in then?' she asked.

'Yeah. You goin' to drop it in for me?'

'Why always me?'

'You know why?'

'Tell me – why have they all got it in for you?'

'They're jealous.'

'Of what?'

'My dad and his bread for starters.'

'But why join if they're all goin' to be dead nasty to you? Who wants to join their rotten club anyway?'

'I do.'

'Why?'

'I don't like to be beaten, do I?'

'But while they're running things they'll make life hell for you.'

Bernie paused. Then he said, 'Maybe they won't be runnin' things for very much longer.'

'What's that supposed to mean?'

'It means what it says. I'm tellin' you – there's going to be big changes on the United scene. And when they start to happen – that lot won't know what's hit 'em. I can't wait for that.'

Becky looked at Bernie and saw the vengeance in his eyes. It was not a side to his character that she had seen before.

When Boxer got down to the club-house, Sheila, Jenny, Gerry, Gonk and Wurzel were all watching the Prof count out last night's disco takings on to the table.

'We took fifty-four on the door, right?' said the Prof.

'Right,' said Wurzel.

'Ten quid in the bar – and seven pounds twenty on the raffle. That makes a grand total of – seventy-one pounds and twenty pence altogether.'

'We're rich,' said Wurzel excitedly. 'What are we gonna spend it all on?'

'We could put it in the bank,' said Jenny.

'No way,' said Wurzel. 'We didn't go to all this trouble just to stick it in the bank, did we?'

Then Boxer said, '*I'll* tell you what I think we should do with it. But I don't know how many of you lot will agree with me.'

'Go on,' said Gerry doubtfully.

'I think we should give it to Rasputin.'

There was an incredulous silence, which was finally broken by an outraged Wurzel. 'What? Rasputin uses twenty quid notes to light his fags with.'

'Not any more he doesn't. Not from what Mac's saying. Anyway – it'll help to buy some new players. We need 'em.'

'And what's seventy-one quid gonna do?' asked Wurzel. 'Who can we buy wi' that? Ossie Ardiles or Glenn Hoddle?'

'Look,' said Boxer. 'I'm tellin' you – the club's really feeling the pinch. Mac was dead keen to sign Joey Collins, and Rasputin reckons we haven't even got the twenty grand to buy him with.'

Jenny said, 'Hasn't Wurzel got a point? I mean – even if the club *is* in financial trouble, our miserable seventy-one quid isn't going to make much difference, is it?'

'Every little's bound to help,' said Boxer. 'Anyway – it's the principle, isn't it? Accordin' to Mac, old Cassidy and the Senior Supporters' Club gave the entire takings of their annual dance to the Club.'

There was a protracted and thoughtful silence which was finally broken by Gerry.

'I agree with Boxer,' he said.

Gradually both Gonk and the Prof agreed, but Wurzel said, 'Yeah, well – you would, wouldn't you?'

Sheila intervened in the gathering hostility. 'Let's put it to the vote, then. All those in favour of handing the profits from the disco to Rasputin?'

Every hand went up except Wurzel's. They stared at him

pointedly for a while until, reluctantly, his hand went up.

'The vote's unanimous,' said Sheila. Boxer grinned.

Charlie Russell's Rolls Royce glided to a halt outside United's ground. Charlie was at the wheel and beside him sat Ivor Chalmers, clutching a large briefcase. In the back sat Bernie and Becky.

'Shan't be long, Bernie son,' said Charlie as he got out. 'I'll see you later.' Ivor joined him and they began to walk towards the gate.

'Off you go then,' said Bernie to Becky.

'What did your last slave die of?' she asked.

Bernie gave her the two membership forms. 'You know how it is.'

'I still think it's a waste of time,' she said.

'You trust your old Bernie.'

With exasperation, and clutching the forms, Becky got out of the car. Once she had gone, Bernie leant back luxuriously in the Rolls. Then he pressed a button and a bar unfolded noiselessly. Bernie took out a cigarette, lit it, and leant back again. Life was good – and it was going to get even better.

Mac looked up angrily from his papers as Charlie Russell and Ivor Chalmers marched into his office.

'He's in the gym.'

'Who?' asked Charlie Russell with false innocence.

'The man you're looking for – Rasputin Jones.'

'Thanks.' Charlie and Ivor turned to go and Mac was sure that Ivor was grinning sardonically.

'Mr Russell.'

'Yes?'

Mac's voice was clear and very precise as he spoke. 'Nothing's changed during your welcome absence. This is still my office and I still expect people to knock before they come walking in. Understood?'

But Charlie Russell merely contented himself with a filthy look as he and Ivor beat a hasty retreat.

In the gym, Rasputin, wearing a track-suit, was going through a vigorous work-out.

'That's what I like to see,' said Charlie. 'A young man looking after himself.'

Unenthusiastically Rasputin got off a bicycling machine.

'Rasputin – I'd like you to meet Ivor Chalmers.'

'I've heard a lot about you,' said Ivor obsequiously.

'Nothing good, I bet,' said Rasputin to the accompaniment of Charlie's hollow laughter.

'Look – I'll just take a quick shower and be with you. O.K.?'

A few minutes later Rasputin came back in, wearing a dressing gown and drying his face on a towel.

'You have my attention – for at least five minutes.'

Charlie plunged in. 'Ivor here's into supermarkets in quite a big way. Even owns a chain of 'em.'

'That's nice for him. But what's that got to do with my club?'

Ivor spoke softly. 'I gather you're short of the ready.'

'So are Liverpool and Arsenal.'

'But short to the point of embarrassment. Right?'

'So?'

'So that's why I'm here.'

Becky came into the club-house as Boxer and Gerry were clearing up from the disco.

'Well, well,' said Boxer. 'Look who's here.'

'Can you tell me who I can leave these with?'

'What are they?'

'They're application forms. From Bernie Russell and me.'

'Give 'em to me,' said Gerry.

'He's a nice boy,' said Boxer. 'You can trust him.'

Becky gave Gerry the forms and Boxer a cool look. Then she went briskly out.

'Some people,' said Gerry, 'just won't take no for an answer.'

'It's funny.'

'What do you mean – funny?'

'Six months ago – after what happened, Bernie Russell wouldn't be seen dead around here. Now, because his old man's hanging around, he's got the flamin' nerve to re-apply for membership.'

'Yeah,' said Gerry. 'It's funny all right.'

Bernie was still luxuriously smoking as Becky got back into the Rolls.

'All right?'

'I gave them in.'

'What did they say?'

'Nothing much.'

'Want a fag?'

'No.'

'Never tried one?'

'No.'

'Try one.'

'I said no.'

'Scared?'

'I just don't want to – that's all. Bet your dad wouldn't half be mad if he knew you were smoking.'

'You don't know my dad.'

Bernie drew on his fag, looking knowledgeable, and Becky sat back in the Rolls feeling uneasy.

Back in the gym, Rasputin was getting down to brass tacks.

'So you want to put money into United, right?'

'Yes,' said Ivor. 'You've got it.'

'Why?'

'I might ask you the same question,' returned Ivor craftily.

'Because I'm a nutter. I put it down to all that loud music I used to play. But I wouldn't have thought that was your problem, Mr Chalmers. So come straight with me. Give.'

'It's a simple explanation. I'm a fan. Always have been.'

Rasputin looked at him thoughtfully. 'Oh yes – you'll remember old Baldy Battersby then. Used to nod 'em in from all angles. In fact – they reckoned that was why he wore his hair out so early.'

'Good old Baldy,' said Ivor immediately. 'What a finisher he was.'

'They don't make 'em like him any more, eh?'

'They certainly don't.'

Rasputin looked at Ivor wryly and Charlie, intercepting the look, suddenly felt worried for a reason that he couldn't understand.

'Where's Rasputin?'

'In the gym. But he's busy – having a meeting.'

Boxer frowned. 'I've got some money for him.'

Mac looked up impatiently. 'I told you – he's busy right now.'

Suddenly Rasputin swept into Mac's office. 'Look, I've got to talk –'

But Boxer was still determined to give him the money they had collected at the Disco – the money that he had persuaded Wurzel to give up to the club.

'Look, Rasputin. We collected –'

But Rasputin turned on him brusquely. 'Sorry, old son – I'm up to me neck in it.'

'Come back another time,' said Mac.

Angrily Boxer turned on his heel and went out, hugging the money in an old Oxo tin close to him. What was the point of trying to support the club if they weren't interested? Maybe Wurzel had been right after all – perhaps they should have kept it.

Meanwhile, Mac was reeling back in surprise.

'Half a million quid?'

'That's what he's prepared to bring in.'

'What I couldn't do wi' half a million quid with the players on the market now.'

'Right.'

'What's the catch?'

'Well – for starters he wants seats on the board.'

'Oh yeah.'

'One for him – and one for your friend and mine, Charlie Russell.'

'Why him?'

'They're blood brothers.'

'What did you tell him?'

'Said I'd sleep on it.'

'And what do you think?'

'I smell a rat.'

'Why?'

'Look, Mac – if you had half a million quid, why should you throw it away on United? Just for a free cup of tea and a pork pie in the board room after the matches?'

'No way.'

'So why is he?'

'Football daft?'

'So he says. Reckons he's been a United fan since he was in nappies. Only one problem though – his memory's a bit wonky.'

'How do you mean?'

'I asked him if he remembered Baldy Battersby.'

'So?'

'Do you?'

'No.'

'Neither does anyone else. Because I made him up. But Chalmers remembers him – he used to be his biggest fan.'

Mac burst into laughter. 'What a con man,' he said.

'Like I say – something stinks.'

'It usually does if Charlie Russell's got a hand in it,' pointed out Mac.

'That's true.'

'So what's your decision?'

'The same as before – I'll think about it.'

As Rasputin finally came out into the corridor, he found himself surrounded by the Junior Supporters' Club.

'Hurry on, kids – I'm half an hour late for me next meeting. Give me a chance. Why not come and see me tomorrow?'

While Rasputin vanished down the corridor, Wurzel said, 'As I was sayin' . . .' But Gerry interrupted him.

'Come on – let's go and see Mac,' he said.

They all charged into Mac's office to find him sitting at the desk, looking worried.

'Now what?' he asked, none too graciously.

Gerry gave him the tin. 'Can you give this to Rasputin?'

'What is it – a bomb?'

'Money,' said the Prof.

'Money,' repeated Mac in a slightly glazed way.

'Money we made last night in the disco,' put in Sheila, as if talking to a child.

'And you want to give it to Rasputin?'

'To the club. We heard there were financial problems – and we want to do our bit.'

'How much have you got?' asked Mac.

The Prof said, 'Seventy-one pounds and twenty pence.'

Mac looked up at them with a smile. 'I'll see he gets it,' he said. 'And thanks.'

Slowly the kids walked out, leaving Mac still smiling and staring at the box. Then as other thoughts came into his mind, his smile gradually faded.

Boxer took the forms along to Becky's house himself – hoping that he would see her. He still felt attracted to her – despite the dubious company she kept. So he was delighted when he pressed the bell on Becky's front door – and she opened it herself. But she did not look particularly pleased to see him.

'Hi.'

'Mm?'

'How are you?'

'What do you want?'

'Got a letter for you – from the committee.' He ambled away towards his bike. 'Bernie Russell live next door?'

'Yes.'

'Right – I'll drop his in too.'

Becky tore open her envelope and then, taking care to ensure that Boxer had gone, rushed delightedly round to Bernie's house.

'I'm in,' she said. 'They've accepted me.'

But Bernie only greeted her with a sour face. 'More than they have me,' he said.

Instantly she knew he had been turned down. 'Of course – I'm not joining if they won't have you.'

But Bernie had seen how pleased she was, and somehow he knew that it was not just because of the glories of Dunmore United that she was happy to have joined the club.

'Please yourself,' he snapped. 'I'm busy right now.'

He dismissed her and Becky walked slowly away, down the Russells' garden path and up to her own front door. The houses were set in the best part of town and were roomy and spacious with big gardens. Becky sat down angrily on her front doorstep and put her head in her hands. She felt totally confused.

'Who the hell do they think they are?' Charlie Russell said, crumpling up the letter of refusal. 'They're right little snots. But just wait till I get my feet back under that boardroom table. I'll have 'em out if it's the last thing I do.'

'Has Rasputin accepted the offer yet, Dad?' asked Bernie angrily.

'Not yet. But he will. Then I'll sort them all out – including high and mighty Mac Murphy.'

The telephone rang and Bernie answered it. He came back grinning. 'It's Rasputin for you, Dad.'

'Aha,' said Charlie with a confident ring to his voice. 'Hallo, Rasputin, old son.' But as he listened his smile turned to a look of contorted anger. 'You're kidding. You have to be kidding. You're turning down half a million without even putting it to the board. You're mad.'

Charlie banged down the phone and turned to an alarmed Bernie, who said, 'They can't have turned it down, Dad.'

Charlie yelled at him. 'Why don't you shut up?'

With that, he hurried out of the room.

Boxer was training on the punchball in the school gym when Becky Marsh entered. He paused to grin at her but she did not return it. Instead she said, 'You think you're funny, don't you?'

'Funny?'

'You know what.'

'Oh, I see. Well – we told you he wouldn't get in.'

'You can't keep him out just because you don't like him.'

'It's nothing to do with what I feel about him,' began Boxer indignantly.

'Of course it's not,' she returned sarcastically.

'It's the decision of the whole committee – and it was a unanimous one. We don't want him in because he's a troublemaker *and* a thief. He tried to stitch me up with the police and I nearly ended up in court. That's the sort of bloke he is.'

'Well, that's your version.'

'Eh?'

'I heard Bernie's.'

'Go on then. What did *he* say?'

'He told me you did the Supporters' Club over and nicked some bottles – and then got him blamed for it.'

Boxer stared at her, speechless.

'That's a lie. I tell you it was 'im who tried to get *me* blamed.'

'Well – you *would* say that, wouldn't you?'

She walked hurriedly out of the gym, leaving Boxer staring after her. Then with an angry movement he returned to the punchball and began to beat hell out of it.

That evening Derek Cassidy paid a visit to Charlie Russell's house. Charlie gave him an over-enthusiastic welcome.

'Derek. Come in, my old mate.'

He closed the sitting room door and Bernie, who was hanging around on the landing, inched down the stairs so that he was in a good position to eavesdrop. Meanwhile, in Charlie's living room, Ivor Chalmers slowly rose from a chair to greet Derek Cassidy.

'Ivor Chalmers – Derek Cassidy. Derek's Chairman of the Supporters' Club and Ivor runs Chalmers Foods.'

Charlie began to dispense drinks as he talked.

'Now if it wasn't for Derek and all the work he's put in over the years, there wouldn't be a Dunmore United.'

Cassidy, obviously flattered, said, 'I wouldn't pitch it quite as strongly as that.'

'And modest with it,' said Charlie, pouring himself a large scotch.

Just at that moment the doorbell rang and Bernie raced to answer it, annoyed to be distracted from his eavesdropping. Irritably he opened it, saw Becky on the threshold, grabbed her and with a hand to his lips, drew her towards his listening post.

In the sitting room, Charlie was saying, 'Now I'm going to be frank with you, Derek. We've asked you round here to pick your brains.'

'If I can be of any service,' said Derek Cassidy, demurely sipping at his scotch.

40

'We believe you can. But first of all I want to ask for some advice about my lad Bernie.'

'Oh yes,' said Derek a little doubtfully.

'Your Junior Supporters' Club –'

'Hang on. It isn't *mine*. They're a group that operates quite independently of my Supporters' Club.'

'The point is – they're putting a block on my lad joining 'em.'

'Oh dear,' said Derek weakly. 'There always seems to be trouble with that lot.'

'You don't approve of them, Mr Cassidy?' asked Ivor blandly.

'Whether I approve of them or not doesn't count, Mr Chalmers. They're the protégés of our beloved manager.'

'I know that all too well,' smiled Charlie. 'Now what we want to tell you is this. Mr Chalmers and I have every reason to suppose that we'll be having a bigger say in club affairs in future.'

'Oh yes?'

'We feel, like you obviously do, that the Junior Supporters' Club is promoting entirely the wrong image for the club – and we'd like to do something about that.'

'I see.'

'We'd like to turf the lot of them out. Then we'd leave you to run your own Junior Section in your own way.'

'Well,' said Derek Cassidy with sudden enthusiasm. 'That would be something. And not before time in my opinion.'

'Ours too. So that will come. But before that happens there was something we thought you might be able to help us with.'

'If I can I'd be delighted.'

'Rasputin Jones is, I believe, the major shareholder in the club. Am I right?'

'You are.'

'But what I want to know is what kind of holding does he

have? In other words – does he own more than fifty-one per cent of the shares?'

'I've no idea – but there's an easy way to find out. There's a list of all shareholders and their holdings in the office.'

'Is there indeed?'

'Yes.'

'Well – fancy that now.'

A few moments later, Becky was looking at Bernie with puzzled eyes.

'Could they really disband the club?' she whispered.

'Course they could,' hissed Bernie. 'If they were on the board, that is. Then old Cassidy could start up a new club – and we'd be in and Boxer and Co. would be out. Right out. Cassidy can't stand any of 'em.'

Suddenly they heard Charlie and Derek Cassidy emerging from the living room and they both ducked back, out of sight.

'Thanks for coming round, Derek,' said Charlie as he showed him out. When he walked back into the sitting room, Charlie treated Bernie to an enormous wink.

Outside, Becky turned and whispered to Bernie. 'You really hate their guts, don't you?'

'You said it. I really hate their guts.'

Becky continued to stare at Bernie.

'What's the matter?'

'Nothing.'

'Come on. Let's make some coffee.'

Bernie strode into the kitchen and Becky followed slowly. She was gradually learning more and more about Bernie's hatred, and she didn't like it one bit.

Ivor and Charlie Russell faced each other across the fireplace of the Russells' living room.

'There's just the one problem,' Charlie was saying. 'If

we're going to mop up all the spare shares and kick Rasputin out we must look at that list.'

'Well,' said Ivor. 'We can hardly go to Murphy and ask him for it.'

'So?'

'We'll just have to think of another way of having a look at it.' Ivor's pale eyes met Charlie's. They understood each other.

Later that evening, in the club-house of the Junior Supporters' Club, Gerry handed Boxer a letter.

'What's this?'

'It's from Becky. Telling us what we can do with the club.'

'It's her loss – not ours.' But Boxer was visibly annoyed.

Sheila, who was behind the tea bar, said, 'I still don't get it.'

'Get what?' asked Gerry.

'I've chatted to her at school and she seems a nice kid. Why does she hang around with a creep like Bernie Russell?'

'They live next door to each other,' said Boxer in a gloomy voice. 'I s'pose that's how they got to know each other.'

'Anyway,' said Sheila, 'I'm off now.' She turned to Gerry. 'You ready?'

'Can you manage the rest of the clearing up yourself?' asked Gerry.

'I'll do it,' said Boxer. 'You get off now.'

They said good night and Boxer began putting away the last of the coke cans under the bar.

Sheila and Gerry passed Mac as he was leaving his office.

''Night, Mac,' said Sheila.

'Is Boxer still in the club?' asked Mac.

'He's clearing up,' said Gerry.

'O.K. See you.'

''Night.'

They went their separate ways and the ground was quiet. Then the man stepped into view. He was in his thirties, well-built, and had a very definite sense of purpose. He came out of a car parked further down the street and in his hand was a bunch of keys.

Mac looked into the club-house before he went.

'Ready for home, squire?'

'Not yet. You go on – I'll walk home.'

'O.K. But don't go getting yourself mugged or anything.'

Boxer grinned and squared up to Mac. 'I can look after myself, Mac.'

'I know you can. See you later.'

Mac hurried out, leaving Boxer still tidying up.

The man circled in the shadow of the offices, looked around him, and then began to work hurriedly at the lock. After a few moments of feverish activity, the door opened and he slipped into the corridor. Walking softly and carefully up the broken lino, he came to the office door, where he hesitated. Then he tried the door – and found it locked. With sudden decision he drew a heavy spanner out of his pocket and broke the frosted glass. Then, cautiously, he reached a hand through the jagged hole and opened the door.

Boxer was crossing the forecourt when he heard the sound of breaking glass. He paused, listening, almost unable to believe what he had heard. Then he turned and walked up to the main door. It was open. Boxer paused and slipped quickly inside. He then walked slowly and softly along the darkened corridor until he saw a light.

With the aid of a torch, the man worked swiftly and professionally through the filing cabinet. After a while, he found what he wanted. Carefully checking to make sure that it was the right document, he slipped it into his pocket. Then he froze, for his trained ears could make out a tiny sound in the corridor. Hurriedly snapping off his torch, he darted behind the door. Once hidden, he stood poised, tense, ready.

Boxer stood looking at the smashed glass in the office door, the hairs on the back of his neck literally rising. He had never known the sensation before and for a moment almost laughed aloud at the truth of the old saying. Then his stomach began to churn and he felt sick. But Boxer was determined not to give in to his fear, and with sudden decision, and legs that felt like jelly, he pushed the door open and went warily inside. For a moment he stood in the darkened office, feeling the raw animal fear. Then the heavy spanner descended on his neck with unbelievable force and Boxer fell into a void of intense pain followed by utter darkness.

Clutching the document and not pausing to give a second glance to Boxer's crumpled body on the floor, the man raced from the office, down the corridor and out of the building. Glancing around and breathing heavily, he then began to walk slowly towards his car.

Ivor Chalmers sat behind the steering wheel of the Rolls Royce in a lonely car park on the edge of town. It was after eleven and he frequently glanced at his watch. Then the other car pulled quietly into the park and drove up to the Rolls. A man got out and casually walked over.

A patch of moonlight wanly illuminated the blood on Boxer's head. Returning consciousness made him moan feebly but he did not move.

*

'Did you get it?'

'Yeah.'

The man handed Ivor the register of shareholders' names. 'Good lad.'

As Ivor reached for his wallet, the man said quietly, 'Something happened.'

Elaine switched off the television and turned to Mac.

'It's after eleven. He should have been home by now.'

'He probably called in at the Chinese chippy.'

'He still should have been home by now.'

Mac looked at her, sighed, and rose from his armchair to fetch his coat. Elaine did the same.

'Now look –' began Mac.

But she was firm. 'I'm coming with you – whether you like it or not.'

Boxer stirred again. His neck felt like a leaden weight and he had a splitting headache. He tried to move, but the pain was so intense that he slumped into unconsciousness again.

As Mac's car came to a halt outside the offices of Dunmore United, he noticed that the door was open. He turned to Elaine.

'Stay here,' he said. Then he silently left the car and began to walk towards the door. A few seconds later he was moving quietly down the corridor. Then he came to the smashed glass and paused. With sudden resolution, Mac moved forward.

Elaine waited impatiently in the car, her mind a jumble of confused thought. Then she heard Mac's voice.

'Elaine, come quickly.'

With the fear rising in her, Elaine jumped out of the car and ran towards the dark shadow of Mac.

'Oh, my God.'

They both knelt beside the still unconscious form of Boxer.

'Somebody's clobbered him,' said Mac.

'Is he all right?'

'I don't know, but don't touch him. Ring for an ambulance. Quickly.'

'Simpson – you're a flaming idiot.' Ivor was furiously raging at the man who sat beside him in the front seat of the Rolls.

'He surprised me – coming in like that.'

'What state was he in when you left him?'

'I didn't stop to look, did I?'

'Get out.'

'Where's the money?'

'You reckon you've earned it?'

The man sat there unmoving, and finally Ivor Chalmers took an envelope out of his pocket and threw it at him.

'Now get out.'

Hurriedly the man left the Rolls, walked across to his own car and drove off, gunning the engine. Ivor then picked up the telephone and, with a shaking hand, began to dial. It rang once – and was immediately picked up.

'Yeah?' Charlie Russell's voice was tense.

'I thought I'd let you know that I managed to get my hands on a copy of the United share register.'

'That's great.'

'We'll talk tomorrow.'

'Everything O.K.?'

'I said we'll talk tomorrow.'

Bernie looked up at his father quizzically as Charlie thoughtfully replaced the phone.

'Good news, Dad?'

'I should say so. I'll tell you this, son – when Ivor Chalmers takes something on he doesn't mess about.'

★

'Did you get the police?'

Elaine was sitting in the corridor outside a door marked Ward 3 as Mac came striding down the corridor.

'I left them down at the club with Rasputin. Any news?'

'Not yet.'

But just at that moment the door of the ward opened and a doctor emerged.

'My name's Dr Wallace. Are you the boy's parents?'

'He's staying with us,' said Elaine agitatedly. 'His parents are in Kuwait.'

'How is he?' demanded Mac.

'He's going to be all right. But he'll have a thick head for a few days.'

'Thank God,' said Elaine. All the colour had drained from her face and she was shaking from head to foot. Mac put his arm around her.

'Can we see him?'

'See him for a couple of minutes. Then he'd better sleep.'

Elaine hurried towards the door of the ward and Mac followed her.

'Thanks, Doc,' he said.

'He's a tough boy.'

'You can say that again,' returned Mac. The doctor could see the tears in the big man's eyes as he hurried inside.

Boxer's face was very pale as he lay propped up against the pillows.

'Wotcha.'

'Hallo, love. How do you feel?' asked Elaine.

'Like I've been hit with a blunt instrument. But I'll be O.K.'

'What the hell happened?' asked Mac.

Boxer spoke slowly. 'I was on my way home, right? Soon after you left.'

'Right.'

'I was passin' the office and I noticed the door was open. I

48

went to close it – then I thought I heard something coming from your office. I went in to have a look and the next thing – the lights went out.'

'What are you?' exploded Mac. 'Some kind of thicky or something?'

'Eh?'

Elaine intervened indignantly. 'Mac!'

Mac turned on her angrily. 'He could have been killed going in there like that. Who the hell did you think you were? James Bond or somebody?'

'The Saint, I think,' returned Boxer.

'That's the way it could just have worked out, son,' said Mac grimly.

'I think you were very brave,' put in Elaine softly.

'Also very daft,' Boxer's voice was weak but certain.

'So next time you come across somebody trying to burgle a place, forget the heroics. Find a call box and dial 999.'

'Always assuming, of course, that some vandal hasn't ripped the phone out,' added Elaine.

'I mean it, Boxer,' said Mac. 'I'm responsible for you. And when your mother and father come back in six months I intend to deliver you back to them safe and sound. And certainly not with holes in your head. Do you hear me?'

'Yes, boss,' said Boxer.

'How's your head now?'

'Like I went for a high cross. And mistimed it a bit.'

'I know the feeling. It used to happen to me all the time. In fact, that's one of the reasons I decided to go into management instead.'

'Go on. Bet you weren't 'alf as rubbish as you're always goin' on you were.'

'True. All true,' said Elaine.

'Thanks,' replied Mac.

'When can I come home?' asked Boxer with impatience.

'Well,' said Mac. 'That depends. They got this very nasty shock when they saw the X-rays of the inside of your head.'

'Oh, yeah?'

'All they could find was this notice inside. "Watch this space"!'

Boxer grinned across at Elaine and some of his dead pallor seemed to lift.

'Sympathetic type, isn't he?'

'Always has been,' she replied.

'Doesn't make no sense, breaking into this place,' said Rasputin with his feet up on Mac's desk, puffing at a large cigar. 'My office over at the rink, yeah. If only for the booze and the cigars. But not this place.'

Mac and Elaine faced Rasputin, staring at him quizzically. They were just as much at a loss as he was. Then there was a tapping at the door and Sheila, Wurzel, Gonk and Gerry came charging in.

'We just heard about Boxer,' said Gerry. 'How is he?'

'Well,' said Mac. 'He's got a damn great lump on his head, but apart from that the word is he'll probably live.'

'Is he at home?' asked Sheila.

'No,' said Elaine. 'He's still up at the hospital.'

'Can we visit?'

'Do you seriously think anyone in their right mind's going to let you lot into a hospital?' asked Mac.

But Elaine said, 'I'm sure you can go in. He's in Ward 3.'

'Thanks, Elaine,' replied Sheila and without further questions the bunch of them roared off.

When they had gone, Rasputin said angrily, 'What the 'ell did they think they was going to find? Our revolutionary new attackin' formation for the first match on Saturday?'

'When we came in here,' said Mac, 'the second drawer of the filing cabinet was open.'

'Is anything missing?'

'I'll need to check,' said Elaine.

'Then let's check right away. Meanwhile – how's the kid?'

Elaine replied, 'They said he was comfortable when I rang this morning.'

'And you'll be going to see him later?'

'This afternoon.'

'Then give him this record token from me.' Rasputin shoved it across the desk and before either of them could thank him he said, 'I mean – you never know. He might just show a bit of good taste and spend it on one of my old albums.'

'Bit of a sale of golden oldies on, is there?' asked Mac.

With a sardonic grin, Rasputin left, leaving both Mac and Elaine realizing how much he could really care.

Sheila, Gonk, Wurzel and Gerry stood in the corridor outside Ward 3 and wondered what they were going to do next.

'Do we just walk in?' asked Gonk hesitantly.

'Why not?' replied Wurzel with sudden resolution. Boldly he opened the door and walked straight into a formidable-looking West Indian ward sister. Wurzel could see Boxer in bed behind her, sitting up and reading a comic.

Wurzel said, 'Hallo.'

'Yes?' replied the sister.

'We was just visitin' Boxer.'

'Boxer?' asked the sister in frosty tones.

'Him over there,' hissed Wurzel.

The sister folded her arms. 'Not at this time of day you aren't. Visiting is between three and four and seven and eight.'

'Oh, come on, nurse,' said Gonk desperately. 'We've spent nearly half an hour getting here.'

'Then spend another half an hour getting back. And for your information it's sister. Now out – all of you.'

She hustled them outside and sulkily but obediently they went.

Back in the corridor, they held a hurried, whispered conference.

'I can't come back tonight,' said Sheila. 'I've got a guitar lesson.'

'Neither can I,' returned Gerry disconsolately.

'There must be some way we can see him,' whispered Gonk.

'Hang on a minute,' replied Gerry. 'I've got an idea.'

He set off down the corridor and the others dutifully followed. Eventually Gerry led them out into the grounds, where he paused.

'I just realized – the windows of Boxer's ward look out on the main gates.'

'So –' Gonk looked at him blankly.

'Those are the main gates over there – which means *this* must be the ward.'

'Good thinkin', Boy Wonder,' said Gonk and they made their way cautiously across the grass towards the windows of the ward. With equal caution they peered through the window, only to see the West Indian sister on the telephone. Then she put it down and looked towards them. With incredible speed they all ducked down behind the window-sill. They crouched there for some time. Then, they very slowly raised their heads again, peered through the window and saw that she had gone.

'Come on,' said Gerry. 'Now's our chance.'

He led them towards a door that opened onto the ward. Gerry tried the handle, found that it was open, and they all filed furtively inside.

'Hi.'

Boxer looked up from reading *Roy of the Rovers* in amazement.

'How the 'ell did you get in here?'

Wurzel began, 'Well – it wasn't easy. But once I'd put my brain to the problem . . .'

'What brain?' asked Gerry.

'How are you, Box?' asked Gonk solicitously.

'I've got this big crater in me 'ead.'

'That's where it comes from then,' said Gerry.

'What?' Boxer was still a bit shaky and he felt they were being a bit too boisterous for him. But he was very pleased to see them all the same.

'All this sawdust all over the floor.'

'Funnee,' said Boxer. 'Very funnee.'

But Wurzel was determined to continue the vigorous fun. 'Lucky they only hit him on the 'ead. And not somewhere where it would have really hurt.'

'Did you see who it was hit you?' asked Sheila.

'No I didn't.'

As they talked, Wurzel helped himself to grapes at the side of the bed.

'Do help yourself to a grape,' said Boxer. 'I mean – don't wait to be asked, will you?'

'Thanks,' said Wurzel, offering one to Gonk.

'Try to leave just a few,' said Boxer. 'Just in case I have any other visitors.'

'They'll probably bring you some more,' put in Gerry sympathetically. He also began to join in the grape orgy. Boxer lay back in bed smiling.

'Don't look now – but *you* have a visitor.'

Slowly they all turned to confront the West Indian sister. Very quickly Wurzel said, 'You ain't gonna believe this – but we got lost.'

'You're right,' she said. 'I don't. So get lost again. Out!'

Reluctantly they all left, reassuring Boxer that they would all see him again soon. Once they had gone, the sister turned to Boxer.

'Friends of yours?'

'Fans,' he replied. 'They just can't manage without me.'

The sister picked up an armful of clothes and dropped them on the bed. The clothes looked familiar.

'What's going on?' asked Boxer.

'They're called clothes,' said the sister. 'Everyone's wearing them these days. You ought to try them. Or were you thinking of going home in your pyjamas?'

'Terrific,' said Boxer, leaping out of bed and beginning to unbutton his jacket. Then he noticed that the sister was making no attempt to leave him.

'Er –'

She looked at him wryly, shook her head and pulled a screen around the bed for him. Behind it, Boxer began to sing.

Bernie Russell was sitting on the wall that divided the Marsh and Russell back gardens. Becky was sitting on a bench.

'You going to the match on Saturday then?' she asked.

'No.'

'It's the first match of the season.'

'Dunmore United's a load of rubbish.'

'They've been a lot better since Mac Murphy took over.'

'Never won nothing, have they? He's just an old Fourth Division scrubber. He doesn't know nothin'.'

'Did you hear what happened down at the club last night?'

'What?'

'Somebody broke into the office, didn't they?'

'Probably the England manager, lookin' for players. I don't think.'

'One of the kids from the Junior Supporters' Club surprised the burglar and got clobbered.'

'Who?'

'Boxer Reed – according to a couple of girls from school.'

'Great stuff. Something serious I hope.'

Becky looked up at him, startled and shocked. 'You hope?'

'Course I hope.'

'Bernie – he could have been seriously hurt.'

'Was he?'

'No – luckily.'

'Pity.'

She stared up at him angrily. 'What a terrible thing to say.'

'Look.' He spoke slowly as if she was stupid. 'He hates my guts – I hate his.'

'It's still a terrible thing to say.'

'Look, I thought you felt the same way about him as I do.'

'I still wouldn't wish him any harm,' protested Becky indignantly.

'I would,' replied Bernie. 'Any time.'

Bernie heard the sound of the front gate opening and from where he was sitting he could see Ivor Chalmers coming up the front path. A thoughtful look crossed Bernie's face.

'See you later,' he said to Becky. Bernie jumped down from the wall into his own back garden and made his way into the house. He wanted to eavesdrop on the conversation that Ivor was going to have with his dad. But Bernie left Becky with very troubled thoughts indeed.

Ivor opened his brief-case and pulled out of it the United share register. Leaning on the mantelpiece, Charlie Russell grinned.

'How did you manage it?'

'Doesn't matter. What does matter is we've got it. And what matters even more is that we're right about Rasputin's holdings.'

'Are we now?'

'Now he certainly owns the major shareholding in the club. But he doesn't hold anything like fifty per cent.'

'Which means,' said Charlie slowly, 'that if we can mop up the rest of the shares . . .'

'We're in, and he's out.'

'Terrific. Now what's the first step?'

'We need what's called a catspaw.'

'A catspaw?'

'That's right.' He smiled at Charlie. 'Somebody to front for us. Somebody who probably knows most of the share-holders personally. Somebody who can be trusted to do the dirt on both Rasputin Jones and Mac Murphy. If it was made worthwhile enough for him, that is.'

Charlie nodded his head and winked. 'That's funny. I know the very bloke.'

'Mr Cassidy?' Elaine said into the phone. 'No – I'm afraid he's not here at the moment, Mr Russell. Any message? Right – I'll tell him you called. 'Bye.'

She put down the phone and there was a tap on the window. Looking up she saw no one. Then there was another tap, and looking up, Elaine saw Boxer's grinning face.

'Boxer!'

Elaine ran to open the door and suddenly Mac appeared behind him.

'You should be at home in bed,' said Elaine.

'The doctor said I could get up – if I have an early night tonight.'

'How's your head?'

'Muzzy.'

'Do you want some coffee?'

'Great.'

'Well – plug the kettle in then!'

Elaine turned to Mac. 'I've got something to show you.'

'Oh, aye?'

She produced a file marked 'Share Register' and handed it to Mac.

'What's this?'

'It's an empty file.'

'So?'

'It shouldn't be. I had it out only last week checking some addresses and I know I put it back. I also keep it in the drawer we found open.'

'What are you suggesting – that this was what the burglar was after?'

'Nothing else seems to be missing.'

'O.K.,' said Mac. 'If anyone wants me I'll be at the ice-rink seeing Rasputin.'

'O.K., love. But what do you think about . . .'

'I want to think. I want to do a lot of thinking.'

With that enigmatic statement, Mac strode out.

Twenty minutes later, Mac was having coffee with Rasputin. Lighting a cigar and leaning back, Rasputin said, 'Who the 'ell would want to nick the share register?'

'Somebody obviously did.'

'But there's no point, mate. I mean – a copy of the register's kept in an office in London and for a few pence any member of the public has the right to look at it. I just don't buy it. I think our friend just grabbed the first thing he came across when the kid surprised him – and scarpered.'

Mac said nothing, but simply stared ahead abstractedly.

'So,' said Rasputin. 'If you've now finished your father figure act of running to and from the hospital, let's talk about something important, shall we? Like how we're going to stick six in on Saturday and embark on our triumphant march to promotion this season. Eh?'

'Yes,' said Mac slowly. 'Let's do that.'

The next day was a Saturday and there was a good crowd at the turnstiles of Dunmore United. Inside the club-house, Sheila and Jenny were serving drinks while Gonk and Wurzel ran the shop. Half a dozen boys and girls of a similar age were examining the goods on sale, and among them, looking rather out of place, was Derek Cassidy.

'Can we sell you anything, Mr Cassidy?' asked Wurzel.

'Hardly,' came the reply.

'Then what can we do for you?' asked Gonk bluntly.

'I'm just checking that everything's in order, that's all – and passing on to you a message from Mr Jones – that he doesn't want any repetition of last season's outbreak of violence in here.'

'That wasn't our fault,' said Wurzel defensively.

'Of course not,' said Cassidy sarcastically. 'It never is, is it? So just remember – you have been warned.'

Suddenly the dog, which was sitting under the table, began to growl at him.

'And kindly keep that animal under control as well.'

'Don't worry,' said Gonk. 'He won't hurt you, Mr Cassidy. He knows you're our friend.'

'And less of the cheek as well,' said Cassidy, with attempted dignity.

The dog growled again and Derek Cassidy abruptly left. As he went, Jenny came over from the tea bar.

'You know what he's really doing, don't you?'

'What?' asked Wurzel innocently.

'Being nosey. To see if we're selling stuff at our shop cheaper than they are at theirs.'

'Which we are.'

They all laughed and then Jenny said, 'Just look who's here.'

Becky Marsh came hesitantly into the club-house, trying to pretend she was just looking at the goods like the rest of the Junior Supporters' remaining customers.

'Can we sell you anything?' asked Wurzel.

'How much are the badges?' she asked.

'To you – 50p. And at that price I'm giving 'em away.'

'I'll take this one.'

'Right.'

Becky gave Wurzel 50p and put the badge into her coat.

'Can I get a drink here?' she asked.

'Strictly speaking you can't,' said Jenny, 'seeing that you're not a member.' Then she softened. 'But we'll make an exception in your case.'

Becky followed Jenny gratefully over to the tea bar, where she bought a coke. For a while she stood there drinking it. Then, with a rush, Becky Marsh finally told them why she had come.

'Er – is it true that one of you lot got hit over the head by a burglar the other night?'

'Yeah,' said Sheila. 'Boxer.'

'Was it bad?'

'He had to go to hospital. But he's out now. He might be in any moment.'

At once Becky turned to go, but Sheila, after a quick look at Jenny, said, 'Can I tell you something you should know?'

'What?'

'I don't know what Bernie Russell told you about Boxer, but I'll promise you it was a pack of lies,' said Sheila softly.

'Yeah?'

Sheila continued determinedly. 'Boxer's never done a thing to him and that's the truth. It was the other way round.'

But Becky was not so easily convinced. 'You would say that, wouldn't you. You're a friend of his.' Swiftly Becky turned to go, but walked straight into Boxer at the door.

'Hi,' he said. But Becky simply gave him a strange look and walked out. Boxer went over to the girls.

'What's she want then?'

'She's been making a few inquiries,' said Jenny.

'About your health,' said Sheila.

'What?' asked Boxer disbelievingly, and both girls collapsed into giggles.

There was a good crowd at the ground, noisy, good-natured and, above all, enthusiastic.

'We want three. We want three.'

The kids of the Dunmore United Junior Supporters' Club chanted the words fervently on the terraces as the ball came into the box and, to their jubilation, a United striker hammered it into the net. The kids went wild.

'Easy. Easy.'

Just then the referee blew for time and the kids went wild again. Dunmore had won for the first time in months and Rasputin gave the thumbs-up to Mac, who, rising from his bench, looked delighted. It was a good day for Dunmore – a day Mac had been waiting for for a long time. He felt elated and optimistic about the future.

Derek Cassidy was standing outside the changing room as the weary but triumphant team came through.

'Well done, lads,' he said, patting them on their backs. 'That's the stuff to give the troops. Good adventurous football. That's what we want.'

Mac and Rasputin came in together.

'I'll see you later,' said Mac.

'Right – go and give 'em a big pat on the back from me.'

Mac went inside the dressing room to congratulate his players. But as Rasputin headed towards the board room and a brandy, he was stopped by Charlie Russell.

'Well?'

'I just want you to know that offer is still open – if you decide to change your mind.'

'Forget it, mate.'

'I'm sure –'

'I said – forget it.' Rasputin disappeared and Charlie, seeing Derek Cassidy still hovering by the dressing room door, hurriedly went up to him. Charlie Russell hated being snubbed – and Rasputin had just snubbed him very effectively.

'Derek. Good to see you.'

'And you, Charlie.'

'Look Derek – why don't you come round to the house tonight? We've got a little proposition to put to you.'

'Well –'

61

''Bout seven?'

'Yes. All right then. Yes.'

'Good on you.' Charlie slapped him round the back and hurried out. Derek Cassidy watched him go with an intrigued look on his face.

'How would you like to join the board of United, Derek?'

Bernie Russell flinched as he listened outside to the conversation his father and Ivor Chalmers were having with Derek Cassidy in the sitting room.

'Blimey,' said Cassidy, forgetting to be cool. 'Me – a director?'

'Why not?' said Ivor. 'From what Charlie tells me you do more for the club than anyone else down there.'

'But how – how can you get me on to the board?'

Charlie said, 'We will do. That I can guarantee. But you have to perform a little service for us first. And with your contacts it won't be difficult.'

'I don't –'

Charlie Russell tossed Cassidy the share register. 'Now, that's the share register, that is. What we want you to do is make contact with everybody on there who owns as much as a single share – and offer to buy it at twice the share value.'

'With the exception of Rasputin, that is,' said Ivor. 'He mustn't know anything about it.'

'But – where would I get money like that?' asked the bewildered Cassidy.

'You'll be provided with the money by me. And when you've got your hands on more than fifty per cent, you can make them over to me – at a fat little profit to yourself. Savvy?'

'Yes,' said Cassidy, slowly. 'I savvy.'

'Do you reckon you can do that, Derek?' asked Charlie smoothly.

'I do.'

'And *if* you do – you're guaranteed a seat on the board.'

62

'When do I start?'

'Right now,' said Ivor. 'You've got the nod.'

'We'll be in touch then,' said Charlie, shaking Derek's hand. Taking the hint, Derek rose.

'Goodnight then. I can see myself out – and thanks for the chance.'

He opened the door and Bernie scurried for cover. But once Derek Cassidy was safely out of the front door, Bernie nipped back to his eavesdropping position to hear his father saying, 'One thing, Ivor. Why break in? It was a bit drastic, wasn't it, when you could have got all the stuff at Company House?'

'I tried that. Their copy was out of date. Apparently it happens with a lot of tin-pot clubs like United. They're sometimes years behind.'

'You've taken some risks to get behind the club, Ivor,' said Charlie appreciatively.

But Ivor laughed. 'Come on, Charlie – you don't really think I'm investing all this money in a rubbishy little club like Dunmore, do you?'

'Then what do you want control for?'

'To close it down,' said Ivor blandly.

'What?' asked the amazed Charlie.

'This town is screaming for a centrally based hyper-market, and whoever gets in first will make millions. I intend to get in first – by knocking down the United ground. How about that?'

'How *about* that?' echoed Charlie.

Outside the door, Bernie Russell grinned delightedly. This was revenge indeed. He pictured Boxer's face when he heard the news, and his grin became wider.

Bernie Russell blasted the doorbell of the Marshes' house. Becky opened it angrily.

'Do you have to?'

'You comin' out?'

'I've got homework.'

'Do it later.'

'I don't know about that –'

'Come *on*! They've got this new space invaders down at the old roller rink. It's brilliant.'

Becky hesitated – and gave in. 'Hang on then. I'll just tell Mum where I'm going.'

Bernie Russell waited on the doorstep impatiently. He could hardly wait to tell her his good news.

Rasputin had finally come up with an idea for his redundant roller-skating rink. He had commissioned, practically overnight, a futuristic decor, with science fiction murals on the walls and exotic lighting giving a dim, exciting glow to the banks of space invader machines that lined the walls. The old rink was chock full of kids, and Rasputin stood watching with all the satisfaction of a mother who has recently borne a child – a very vulgar child. Mac stood next to him, amused by the way his dynamic boss had so quickly run up such a money-making proposition.

'Groovy, isn't it?' said Rasputin.

'For your bank account,' replied Mac.

'Don't knock it, mate,' said Rasputin, lighting a particularly fat cigar. 'All these 10ps will buy you a couple of decent players one day.'

'Don't you think it's all a wee bit immoral? Taking money from the kids with these things?'

'Immoral?' rasped Rasputin indignantly. 'Nobody's twistin' their arms. Besides – I'm providing a public service, aren't I? I mean, if they didn't come in 'ere where else would they have to go?'

'And there was me just thinking you were after their cash.'

'The trouble with you, Mac, is that you're a cynic.' He grinned at Mac and then went towards his office. 'See you later.'

'See you.'

Mac paused for a few more seconds, watching the youngsters empty their pockets on the glowing, bleeping machines. Then, as he headed for the door, he met Bernie and Becky coming in.

'All right, Mac?' asked Bernie, with a cheeky grin.

'So you're out of gaol, are you?' he replied. Bernie is all I need, thought Mac as he hurried out of Rasputin's electronic palace.

'Funny man,' said Bernie to Becky. 'But he'll be laughing on the other side of his face when he finds he's out of a job.'

'What do you mean?' asked Becky innocently. 'They all say Mac's the best thing that ever happened to United.'

'Yeah,' said Bernie, 'but there won't be a United much longer, will there?'

He made his way over to one of the machines and began to play. Becky watched him for a couple of minutes with a frown. Then she said, 'What do you mean?'

'What I said.'

'That's stupid.'

'You reckon?' He grinned at her knowingly and moved on to another machine.

'If you mean they'll get thrown out of the Fourth Division – no chance. My Dad reckons with Mac in charge they might even get promoted this time.'

'I don't mean thrown out. I mean just not here any more.'

'How could that happen?'

'Could happen to any soccer club these days,' Bernie said evasively. 'They could just go out of business.'

'But why should that happen to United?'

''Cos it's going to, that's why. Only they don't know it yet. You'll see. But when it does happen, just remember I told you. Right?' He gave her a strange look and went on playing on the machine. But Becky stood behind him, a look of bewilderment spreading over her face. Inside her, another sensation was spreading that at first she couldn't recognize. Then Becky realized it was fear.

The space invader machine belonging to the Junior Supporters' Club of Dunmore United could not have been a greater contrast to those owned by Rasputin. It was heavily beaten up, tarnished and, at the moment, broken down. But, in the club-house, the Prof was doing his best with it. He had taken a panel off and, with a battery of differently shaped screwdrivers, was tinkering with the machinery. He was watched sceptically by Wurzel and Gonk.

'Course,' said Wurzel. 'I think he's a direct descendant of Logie Baird.'

'Did you say Logie Baird or Yogi Baird?' put in Gonk.

The Prof told them to get lost but Wurzel continued mercilessly, 'I mean, I don't know how he can spare the time myself – from workin' on this new missile system he's developin' for the Government.'

'You'll get a missile right up your hooter if you don't buzz off,' snapped the Prof, taking aim with one of his screwdrivers. But he paused as Becky Marsh came in, standing on the threshold, looking nervously at Boxer and Gerry who were playing pool.

'Well, well. Don't look now,' said Gerry. Boxer stopped mid-shot and looked up at Becky.

'Changed your mind about joining the club, have you?' he asked, still leaning over the pool table.

'No. But you know Mac Murphy, don't you?'

'He ought to – he lives with him,' said Gerry.

'What I mean is,' said Becky slowly, 'that if you told him something he'd listen, wouldn't he?'

'Suppose he would,' said Boxer.

'Then I have to talk to you.'

'O.K.'

'Not here though.'

'Right now, I'm in the middle of a game of pool.'

66

'It's important.'

Boxer didn't know what to do. Then he caught sight of Gerry grinning at him.

'I don't mind waiting,' said Gerry. 'I wouldn't like to come between you.'

'Two minutes,' said Boxer, for Gerry's benefit.

'Take as long as you like,' teased Gerry.

Boxer glared at him and then said to Becky. 'Outside – quickly.'

They went out and Gerry immediately started to re-arrange the balls on the table to his better advantage.

'Hey,' said Jenny, coming up behind him. 'That's cheating.'

'No, it's not,' said Gerry. 'It's gamesmanship.'

Boxer and Becky were sitting together in the empty stand. Boxer looked stunned.

'United go out of business? Never. He's barmy.'

'He was dead serious.'

'That's Bernie, isn't it? All mouth and trousers. He's putting you on.'

'Suppose he isn't?' said Becky agitatedly. 'He's heard something – I don't know what. I think Mac Murphy should know.'

'Maybe,' said Boxer. 'Why are you telling *me* all this?'

'Why shouldn't I?' Becky asked belligerently.

'But –'

'Are you going to tell him or not?'

'Yes,' said Boxer still staring at her. 'I'll tell 'im.'

Mac took Boxer seriously but Rasputin was inclined to be dismissive. In Mac's office, Rasputin sneered.

'It's just kids' talk. No more.'

Boxer was determined. 'She convinced me he was serious – that Bernie had heard a whisper.'

'Crazy.'

'I don't know,' said Mac.

'Don't know what?' snarled Rasputin.

'Look – Bernie is Charlie Russell's son. And Charlie does *just* happen to be an associate of Ivor Chalmers. A gent who was trying to buy his way on to the board last week.'

'So?'

'So perhaps he did hear something he shouldn't,' said Mac.

Boxer chipped in. 'Becky says he spends half his time eavesdroppin'.'

'And then,' said Mac. 'There's the other thing we never worked out, isn't there?'

'What other thing?' asked Rasputin. There was a different tone in his voice – one of unease.

Mac spoke quickly. 'Chalmers tried to come it that he was an old United fan. But you said yourself he was obviously lying in his teeth. So if he wasn't – why was he prepared to put half a million in just to get on to the board?'

Rasputin looked at him in exasperation, but he knew Mac had a point. He turned to Boxer.

'You're quite sure that kid hasn't made all this up?'

'I'm sure. She's not like that.'

Rasputin got up. 'I'm going to make a few inquiries. Now.'

He walked quickly out of the room. Mac watched him go with concern – he had never seen his dynamic boss so alarmed.

Boxer joined Becky as quickly as he could get away from Mac. They walked across the forecourt and Becky said, 'What did he say?'

'That Bernie was shooting his mouth off – and it was just kids' talk.'

'He wasn't.' Becky was very upset and they paused.

'Look,' said Boxer. 'You and him are still pretty close. Right?'

'Suppose so.'

'At least, *he* thinks so.'

Becky looked up at Boxer. 'Right,' she said.

'Chat him up some more – see if he'll tell you anything else.'

'All right.'

He looked at her curiously. 'How the 'ell did you come to start going out with him anyway?'

'We live next door and he was the only kid of my age in the road when we moved in three months ago. There was nobody else to talk to.'

'O.K.,' said Boxer. 'Go and talk to him some more.'

Becky felt very uneasy about spying on Bernie Russell but she knew that it was necessary. There was something so revengeful about him that somehow she knew that he was dangerous. So when Bernie borrowed some money from his dad and took her down to Outer Space again, she tried to appear enthusiastic. When they arrived she was nervous, for she could see Gonk, Boxer, Gerry and Wurzel all huddled together by the soft drinks bar in the corner. Nevertheless, Becky knew what was expected of her and she plunged in as Bernie began to spend his dad's money on the machines.

'You know that thing we were talking about yesterday?'

'What thing?' Bernie was intent on his game.

''Bout United going bust.'

'Yeah?'

'You weren't having me on were you?'

'Was I?'

'Weren't you?'

'Course not.'

'But soccer clubs just don't go bust.'

'Why not?' said Bernie, putting more money in. 'They're only businesses, like everything else. And if the blokes runnin' 'em see they're losing money – well, they sell 'em off, don't they?'

'Rasputin Jones wouldn't sell the club for anything.'

'Who says it'll be up to him?'

'But he owns United.'

'For how much longer?' muttered Bernie as the machine bleeped and buzzed in front of him.

Becky turned slightly to catch Boxer's eye – and shook her head.

'I've had a guy dig into Chalmers' past.'

'Oh?'

'And it's messy.'

Mac was sitting in Rasputin's office and he knew that his boss was elated. He was on to something.

'Who've you got digging?'

'A mate from C.I.D.'

'Ah. So Chalmers is bent, is he?'

'Not officially. And I mean by that they've never been able to pin anything on him that would stick. Unofficially they reckon he's been involved in a dozen or so dirty deals and he's always managed to get away with it. What's more, he's built his supermarket empire on the proceeds.'

'I've got a couple of things for you,' said Mac.

'Yeah?'

'Charlie Russell's kid was shooting his mouth off again yesterday. He reckons you won't be owning this club much longer.'

'Does he.'

'And that's not all of it. I've had that sports reporter from the local radio station on the phone. The word is that somebody's been going round mopping up every share in United they can get their hands on. Except the ones owned by you. And guess who's been the buyer?'

'It has to be Russell or Chalmers.'

'Does it?'

'Surprise me then.'

'Cassidy.'

'Give over – he hasn't got that kind of bread.'

'So whose bread is he using then? Because this guy got his information from a very reliable source.'

'No prizes for guessing the answer.'

'Right.'

'So it's Chalmers' bread.' Rasputin was silent for a while. Then he said, 'This friend of yours got any idea about how well Cassidy's doing?'

'The rustle on the grapevine says very well. It stands to reason, doesn't it? Who's going to hang on to shares when the rumour is we're in financial trouble?'

'I'll fix him.' Rasputin began to dial Cassidy's number on the Supporters' Club. After a while, the telephone was answered and Mac heard Rasputin start confidently enough.

'Derek – come up and have a word. Sorry? What! I'll – I'll be down.' Rasputin slammed down the phone, his usual confidence temporarily shaken.

'He wants me to go down to him!' Still stunned, Rasputin hurried out of the office and Mac watched him go. He had never seen him so worried.

Rasputin was calm as he stood over Derek Cassidy.

'I take it the rumours are correct that you've been buying up shares in the club behind my back.'

'There's no law against it, is there?' Cassidy looked confident but underneath that confidence, Rasputin knew there was a frightened little man. Suddenly he felt much better.

'I thought you were a mate,' said Rasputin softly.

'There are times when considerations of friendship have to be set aside,' said Cassidy guardedly.

'Fair enough. But I'm here to tell you that I know who's behind it and you won't get away with it.'

'But Mr Jones – I have.'

'You what?'

Now Cassidy's confidence was gaining on Rasputin's.

'I'm afraid you're no longer the major shareholder in Dunmore United. I am.'

'You've got more shares than I've got?'

'Sixty per cent. We could have picked up more – but they weren't necessary.'

'*We* being Russell and Chalmers.'

'I'm not at liberty to divulge that information at this stage. But you can certainly expect some new faces at board meetings in the future – including mine.'

'You're joking.'

'No.'

'You on the board? You're barmy.'

Left alone, Derek Cassidy suddenly realized that his hands were shaking. He began to chew his fingernails, realizing he was no match for Rasputin. Then he had an idea – an idea that pleased him.

In the club-house, the gang were questioning Becky Marsh about how much she had managed to find out from Bernie. But she had not been that successful.

'She did her best,' said Boxer. 'You can't ask for more than that.'

But just as Boxer finished speaking, Derek Cassidy came marching in, looking extremely pompous.

'Can I have your attention for one moment. Everybody? Thank you. I just thought you might like to know that plans have now been completed for the official formation of a Junior Section of the Senior Supporters' Club. This will be run along proper lines with proper supervision. Membership will be strictly limited and available only with the approval of my committee.'

'Which leaves us out,' said Gerry.

Cassidy smiled. 'All applications will be considered strictly on merit. But it goes without saying that it's hardly going to be open to hooligans, vandals or trouble-makers. This also means, of course, that the establishment of such a section makes the existence of this club quite irrelevant.'

'You can't kick us out just like that.'

'It isn't a matter of anyone being kicked out,' continued Cassidy smoothly. He was enjoying himself – this was easier than dealing with Rasputin. 'We are merely regularizing the situation and bringing into the club the sort of youngsters we're really looking for.'

'Big Mac would never wear that,' said Gerry.

'Big Mac is merely the manager,' said Cassidy with an increasing smile. 'For the moment anyway. But if you'd approached *me* in the first place, none of this sad business would ever have arisen. I must go.'

On his moment of triumph, Cassidy stalked out of the door, leaving the gang to digest the news. For a moment they were silent. Then Boxer said, 'Come on. Let's go and see Mac.'

'There's not a thing I can do about it,' said Mac as he faced the gang across the desk.

'Surely Rasputin can,' said the Prof.

'Listen – Rasputin's no longer in control. Cassidy and his merry men are. Do I have to spell it out? I'll probably be out on my ear before long.'

'I can't believe it,' said Boxer miserably.

'You'd better start trying, son,' said Mac. He stared at Boxer gloomily. All his plans for the future appeared to have been dashed, and it hardly seemed worth carrying on with being the manager of United any longer.

Later on, the gang had a council of war in the club-house.

'There must be *something* we can do,' said Jenny.

'Like what?' asked Gerry hopelessly.

'I dunno, do I?'

'If Rasputin can't do anything – what chance do we have?' asked Gonk.

Then Becky spoke. 'You know the night you got mugged, Boxer?'

'Yeah?'

'You said all that got nicked was a list.'

'The shareholders register,' said Boxer dully.

'A list of everybody who's got shares in the club – and their addresses,' said Gerry in response to Becky's questioning look.

'Only one night,' said Becky, 'I was at Bernie's house and there was a meeting. With Bernie's dad and some other feller.'

'Ivor Chalmers?' asked Boxer.

'I don't know,' she answered. 'Anyway, Bernie was listening – and he got me at it too. Cassidy turned up and they were on to him about some kind of list – a shareholders' list. I remember it now. And he said it would be in Mac's office.'

'What else?' asked Gerry.

'Nothing, except they wanted Cassidy to help them.'

'So you think it might have been Cassidy who whacked you, Boxer?' asked Gerry.

'He wouldn't have the bottle,' commented Wurzel.

'Hang on,' said Boxer. 'If it's like Mac said and it's Cassidy who's been buying up all these shares, he must have been working from some kind of list.'

'And it must have been the one from the office,' said Gerry excitedly. 'Too much of a coincidence for it not to be.'

'That makes the list stolen property,' said the Prof. 'If he's still got it, that is.'

'How the 'ell do we prove that?' asked Boxer.

'If we could get it back – that would be proof,' said Sheila.

'And how do we do that?' asked Gerry.

Gonk grinned. 'It could be in Cassidy's office – if he's been ringing round after people's shares.'

'So it could still be there,' said Jenny.

'He'd be too mean to use his own phone,' put in Wurzel.

Boxer got up. 'Let's go and find out,' he said. 'I'll take a raiding party.'

The gang were tense as they carried out the search. Boxer and Gerry searched Cassidy's office while Wurzel and Gonk stood guard outside the rear door of the Supporters' Club. After a few minutes, Wurzel and Gonk were alarmed to find Derek Cassidy coming briskly around the corner, looking as if he owned the place.

'Just our luck,' muttered Gonk.

Wurzel sprang forward. 'Mr Cassidy.'

'What are you two hanging about for?'

'Waiting to see you, Mr Cassidy.'

'Why?'

'Well, Mr Cassidy,' said Wurzel, raising his voice on the name every time and hoping that Boxer and Gerry could hear him. 'About the Junior Section you were on about.'

'What about it?'

'Do we need membership forms to apply to join?'

'Yeah,' said Gonk, catching on. 'We'd like to apply, MR CASSIDY!'

'They're not ready yet,' returned Cassidy brusquely. 'And I feel it's only fair to warn you that in your case you'd be wasting your time. Not to mention mine. Now clear off.'

He pushed past them and went inside. Wurzel stuck his head round the door.

'We still want to apply, Mr Cassidy.'

Angrily, Cassidy returned. 'I said clear off!' he yelled, and slammed the door in their faces.

'Do you reckon we made enough noise?' asked Wurzel anxiously.

'We couldn't have made any more,' replied Gonk.

Indeed they had made enough noise, for Boxer and Gerry had dived behind the piano immediately. They remained in hiding as Cassidy came into the club bar, emptied a dirty ash tray into a bucket of sand, and then went into his office. Directly he was safely inside, Boxer and Gerry emerged from behind the piano and dashed out. Hearing the noise,

Cassidy immediately came back. But he was too late – there was no one there.

Derek Cassidy settled back behind his desk and lit a small cigar. He looked around him, well pleased with life. He felt power surging over him and a great sense of elation. Then the telephone rang. It was Rasputin.

'I want to see you right away in Mac Murphy's office.'

'I'm a bit tied up, Mr Jones,' said Cassidy smugly. 'Can you pop down here?'

'I should pop up here,' said Rasputin, 'Like now.' He put the phone down at his end, leaving Cassidy clutching the receiver. Then he slowly put it down, rose and went out.

Directly Cassidy entered Mac's office he knew something was up, for not only were Rasputin and Mac there, but Boxer, Gonk, Gerry and Wurzel were there too. Looking taken aback and slightly nervous, Cassidy said, 'You wanted a word?'

'A few,' said Rasputin drily. He threw the share register across the desk at Cassidy.

'Recognize this?'

'It's the share register – of course I recognize it.'

'It was stolen from this office four nights ago,' said Mac. 'Oh?'

'And found a few minutes ago in – one of your office drawers,' said Rasputin.

'How dare you go through my things,' said Cassidy. 'I'll call the police.'

'Don't threaten us with the police,' snapped Mac. 'It's you that's got trouble with them.'

'Me?'

Rasputin chimed in and the gang listened, delighted at Cassidy's growing discomfort.

'When that list was nicked it wasn't just a case of breakin' and enterin'. Boxer here suffered grievous bodily harm.'

'You surely aren't suggesting I was responsible?'

'Why not?' said Mac. 'The list was found in your office.'

'And you've been using it,' said Rasputin, 'to mop up all those shares.'

'It was given to me.'

'By whom?'

'Russell and Chalmers.'

'That's your story,' said Rasputin. 'I've no doubt they'll deny it.' He picked up the phone. 'Let's talk it over with the police.'

'I'm innocent of this,' gabbled Cassidy.

'A crime has been committed,' replied Mac.

'But not by me!' There was a hysterical note to Cassidy's voice now. Rasputin looked at him and put the phone down again.

'Whose name are those shares in right now?'

'Mine.'

'But bought with Chalmers' money.'

'Once I'd got enough – they were to be made over to him.'

'I see,' said Rasputin. 'Well, I'll tell you what, Derek. I'll give you the benefit of the doubt and say I believe that you didn't know the share register was nicked.'

'Thank you,' said Cassidy humbly.

'On one condition – that you sell those shares to me. And *not* at the inflated price you paid for them. At the proper price.'

'But – it isn't my money. You know it belongs to Mr Chalmers.'

'Tell him to take it up with me. Now off you go like a good boy.'

Cassidy turned to go. As he headed towards the door, Rasputin said, 'Oh, and Derek – a word of advice. Keep out of politics – you aren't cut out for it.'

Cassidy hurried through the door and the gang let out a shout of laughter which he heard.

'Aren't you going to boot him out then?' asked Mac.

'Not likely,' said Rasputin. 'Derek's as soft as butter and twice as slippery. But he's the best Chairman the Supporters' Club could have, and United would collapse without him. Besides, he's democratically elected, Mac, and I wouldn't like to renounce that, would I?'

'Of course not,' said Mac laughing.

Charlie Russell and Ivor Chalmers confronted Rasputin in the board room that afternoon. They were furious.

'You'll never get away with it,' said Charlie.

'I already have,' returned Rasputin. 'You're looking at a man who owns eighty per cent of the shares of this club.'

'In that case,' said Ivor, 'you owe me.'

'Do I?'

'Those shares were bought on my behalf at twice the price you paid for them.'

'That's how it is with the share market,' grinned Rasputin. 'Up and down all the time.'

'I'll sue,' raged Ivor.

'So I'll be in one court being sued and you'll be in another explainin' to the coppers how you or one of your heavies broke in here, nicked the register and clobbered a kid.'

'You can't prove that.'

'It's not my job to. It's the police's. And with your track record . . .'

Seeing the hopelessness of his position, Chalmers tried to switch on the charm.

'Look, Rasputin. We're both businessmen and we're both interested in making money.'

'There had to be something we have in common.'

'This town needs a central hypermarket. And this is the place for it – once it's knocked down. We could make a bomb.'

'So that's what it's all about.'

'What do you say, Rasputin?' asked Charlie excitedly. 'You've got the shares, Ivor's got the know-how.'

'I have this thing about lying down with dogs – I might catch fleas.'

'I'll get even with you for this, Jones,' shouted Ivor, losing control.

'A lot of blokes have said that.'

Charlie and Ivor turned on their heels and Rasputin said, 'By the way Charlie, have a word with your kid. He's got big ears and a mouth to match 'em.'

Rasputin followed Charlie and Ivor down the corridor and as they passed Mac, he turned and grabbed them both by their jackets.

'And a further wee word from me, gents,' he said menacingly. 'Get out – and stay out. Or I'll have you both.' He let them go and they hurried past him, visibly shaken. Rasputin grinned and clapped Mac round the shoulders.

'It's just not their day, is it?'

Becky was playing a machine in Outer Space when Bernie came up behind her and grabbed her arm.

'What do you think you're doing?'

'I want a word.'

'You're hurting me.'

'What the 'ell was the idea? Blabbin' to that lot about my dad's plans?'

'Why shouldn't I? Somebody had to stop 'em – they were going to close the club.'

'I got a right good hidin' from my dad last night. Thanks to you.'

He twisted Becky's arm and she cried out.

'Stop!'

Then Boxer's voice came from nearby. 'If you don't want another hidin', drop her arm.'

Bernie turned to find Boxer facing him threateningly. 'I'm not scared of you,' he said defiantly.

'You keep saying that and doing nothin' about it,' said Boxer softly. 'Now do something about it or get out.'

Bernie glared at Boxer and then decided to call it a day. When he had gone, Becky said, 'Thanks.'

'My pleasure – believe me.'

They grinned at each other.

'You comin' down the club then?' asked Boxer.

'When I've finished my game,' returned Becky.

She turned her back on him and continued to play. Boxer stood behind her. He was smiling. She knew that he would wait.

7

There was tremendous relief when the threat to the future of United was over. Mac and Elaine felt secure for the first time, Rasputin was free to stop worrying and concentrate on the fortunes of his new Outer Space video games palace, and the gang settled back into the happy routine that surrounded their membership of the Junior Supporters' Club. But all was not to be calm for very long – how could it be with people like Wurzel around?

Wurzel and Gonk had taken a great liking to Barney, the guard dog Rasputin had brought in to protect the United ground against vandals. They played with him, took him for walks and grew to regard him almost as their own. But Wurzel, despite his love for Barney, was careless and one day while playing with the dog on the forecourt of the club, he was stupid enough to let him run into the path of an oncoming car. Gonk was with Wurzel at the time, and both boys watched horrified as Barney rushed after a stick Wurzel had thrown. The car swerved desperately to avoid the dog. It just missed him but collided instead with a lamp-post, denting the right wing.

'You stupid great nit,' yelled Gonk at Wurzel, and Gonk grabbed the frightened Barney as he came scampering back to them.

'What did you want to go and do that for?' continued the angry Gonk.

'I didn't mean to,' protested Wurzel.

A man had clambered out of the car and was staring angrily down at his dented wing. Then he stared across at Wurzel, Gonk and Barney and with a set and furious face began to walk in their direction.

'Now for it,' said Wurzel.

'And don't be a minute late,' Derek Cassidy was saying to Gerry. 'If you want to go on working here we have a very simple rule. If I'm satisfied with you, I'll help you on. If I'm not, you'll be fired. Understood?' Dutifully Gerry nodded his head, little realizing that Derek Cassidy was only repeating to him what Rasputin had told him about his own new job. Knowing that Cassidy was an efficient creep, Rasputin had put him in as manager of Outer Space. Gerry had applied for a job as assistant at Outer Space for three nights a week – and Rasputin had decided to give him a trial. Cassidy had immediately protested but Rasputin had overruled him, reminding him of his involvement in the recent fracas about the club shares.

'Right,' said Gerry to Cassidy. 'I'll be on time.'

'You'd better be,' replied Cassidy. 'If you're not . . .'

'Yes, I know,' said Gerry. 'I'll be fired.'

'What the hell do you two think you're playing at?' asked Harry Mills, the owner of the damaged car.

'Sorry, mister,' said Wurzel.

'Sorry?' yelled Mills. 'Just look at the state of my new car.'

'He did say he was sorry,' said Gonk.

'And what the devil good is that going to do? I should damn well think he *is* sorry. You kids are an absolute menace round here.'

Barney growled at him, but Mills was not a man to be intimidated by a dog.

'Get out of it,' he shouted at Barney, looking as if he were about to kick him. This was all the provocation the dog needed. With a snarl and a leap, Barney grabbed Mills by the wrist, knocking him to the ground.

'No, Barney!' Gonk grabbed the dog and Wurzel rushed over to Mills.

'Sorry, mister.'

'Get away from me.'

Mills scrambled to his feet, clutching at his wrist.

'That animal's dangerous. He shouldn't be let loose.'

'He thought you were threatening him,' protested Gonk.

'And you did look as if you were gonna kick him,' chimed in Wurzel.

'Your dog?' asked Mills threateningly.

'Belongs to United,' said Gonk.

'Right,' replied Mills. 'Where's the boss?'

Clutching his injured wrist, Mills stood in front of a furiously typing Elaine. 'Are you connected with this so-called football club?' he raged.

'That's one of the reasons I'm doing this typing,' replied Elaine.

'Where's the manager?'

'Here,' said Mac, coming in. 'What can I do for you?'

'That animal out there yours?'

'Which animal?'

'That alsatian the kids are messing about with.'

'Not mine. He could be described as an asset of the club.'

'I've just been savaged by him. Look at this.' Mills showed Mac and Elaine his wrist. The skin had been broken – and there were teeth marks on it.

'My God,' said Elaine. 'He's never done anything like that before.'

'I find that hard to believe,' said Mills sourly.

'He must have been provoked.'

'The only one who's been provoked,' said Mills slowly, 'is me. That dog's just caused me to run into a lamp-post.'

'Look,' said Mac placatingly. 'Let's all calm down. I'll just get the first aid kit and dress that for you.'

'Don't bother. I'll have it seen to properly down at the hospital.'

'Be like that.'

'And I'll tell you this – you haven't heard the end of the matter. Not by a long chalk.'

Mills turned and walked angrily out of the office, leaving Mac and Elaine looking worried.

Wurzel was condemned by almost everyone for playing with Barney so near the road, and Mac was loudest in his protests. Later, a policeman arrived and both Gonk and Wurzel were interviewed. So was Rasputin, who was particularly annoyed when the policeman told him that he would be held responsible for the incident.

'As the owner of the dog, you did entrust it to these young people,' remonstrated P.C. Gibbs.

'I didn't even know they'd taken him out of the ground,' protested Rasputin.

'We take him for a walk every day,' said Wurzel.

P.C. Gibbs turned back to Rasputin. 'With your permission presumably, sir?'

Rasputin glared at Wurzel and Gonk. 'With my permission,' he agreed.

When the policeman had left, Rasputin rounded on the kids. 'You lot had better start working out how you're going to pay for that case,' he announced. ''Cos there's no way I'm going to.'

'Dad.'

Inspector Glossop put down his paper and turned wearily to his son, Wurzel. 'Yeah?'

'Can I ask you something?'

He picked up his paper, saying 'Yeah.'

'Suppose there was this dog.'

'What dog?'

'Just this dog. Nice enough dog. Then one day he bites somebody.'

'Yeah.'

'And this bloke gets all snotty about being bit.'

'He would be, wouldn't he?'

'I mean really snotty. So snotty he tells the fuzz.'

'Fuzz?'

'The police, I mean,' said Wurzel hastily. 'The dog would have to be taken to court.'

'The owner of the dog would. We can't put dogs in the dock.'

'The owner then. Would he be fined if he was found guilty, then?'

'No.'

'So he'd just get a tellin' off?' asked Wurzel eagerly.

'So he would – but that wouldn't be the end of the matter.'

'Oh?'

Inspector Glossop put down his paper. 'One of two things might happen. Firstly he might be ordered to keep the dog under control. Secondly, if the dog had bitten anyone else and the police had a record of it, then the dog might be destroyed.'

'No,' said Wurzel horrified.

His father looked at him in surprise. 'Whose dog are you on about?'

'One at the club. Got into a bit of bother today.'

'I see.' Inspector Glossop picked up his paper again.

'Dad.'

'Now what?'

'You know wings?'

'Angels? A pop group?'

'Wings on cars.'

'What about them?'

'If they get bashed in do they cost a lot to replace?'

Inspector Glossop put down his paper suspiciously. 'Why?'

'I just wondered how much they cost?'

At that moment the doorbell rang and Wurzel jumped up. 'I'll get it.'

He went to the door to find Mr Mills standing there. 'Your parents in?'

'They're away for a few days,' said Wurzel quickly.

But his suspicious father had followed him into the hall. 'What's going on?' he asked.

'Dad,' said Wurzel. 'You're back already.'

'Are you this boy's father?'

'I am.'

'And a policeman! No wonder the country's in such a mess.'

'What's all this about?'

'I'll tell you,' said Mills. 'It's all about my broken wing.' He handed Glossop a piece of paper. 'And how much it's going to cost.'

Rasputin was not in the best of moods as he counted the takings before closing up Outer Space. Knowing he could take advantage of his boss's mood, Cassidy pressed it home.

'Must be rough carrying the can for that dog when you know it wasn't your fault.'

'It is.'

'Never liked the animal myself. He's had a go at me on more than one occasion.' Cassidy paused for effect. 'If you want my opinion, I reckon those kids encourage it.'

'There could be something in that.'

More confident, Cassidy continued. 'A friend of mine got into very similar trouble with a dog of his, you know.'

'Yeah?'

'His dog attacked somebody and he was taken to court.'

'What happened to him?' asked Rasputin morosely, still counting the take.

'It never got that far, actually. In the interim he decided the dog was a menace and had it put down. When the authorities found out, that was the end of the matter. No court case, no appearance, no expense.'

Rasputin looked up at Cassidy thoughtfully. 'Is that so?' he said.

Sweeping up nearby, Gerry overheard the entire conversation. Later, he reported the conversation back to the gang and they all agreed that the situation had become very dangerous.

'I can't believe Rasputin would put Barney down,' said Jenny. 'I mean, he's a bit of a hard case but not rotten like that.'

'They'll have to put me down first,' said Gonk angrily as he went out with Barney. Wurzel followed him miserably. Not only was Barney's future uncertain, but his dad had told him he would have to find the money to pay for Mills' dented wing. And he couldn't think where on earth he could get it from.

'Those kids will be heartbroken if anything happens to that dog,' said Elaine next morning in the office.

'I saw Gibbs at the match,' said Mac gloomily. 'Things don't look too good. They think the dog might have to be put down.'

'Then you've got to do something.'

'What?'

'*You're* the one who usually thinks of something,' said Elaine. 'So start thinking fast.'

Mac sat drumming his fingers on the desk. Then his eyes lit up and he turned to Elaine. 'I've got an idea,' he said.

Mac brought Gonk back with him into the office.

'Sit down,' he said, and Gonk did as he was told.

'I had a talk with that policeman yesterday.'

'Yeah?'

'Mr Mills isn't the first person Barney's bitten. According to the police he attacked someone on a previous occasion.'

'He must have been provoked –'

'That's not important. You can't have dogs running round biting people just because they've been provoked.'

'So you want him put down?'

'I do if Barney's a menace. People are more important to me than dogs.'

'Thanks for your help, Mac.' Gonk got up with a bitter smile.

'Sit down.'

Reluctantly Gonk sat down again.

'Look – if this gets as far as court I wouldn't give much for Barney's chances. There's every chance they could order him to be put down and there's nothing that you or I could do to save him. That is unless Rasputin's got into his head to put the dog down first.'

'So?'

'Suppose Mr Mills withdrew his complaint.'

'Why should he?'

'He might if you went to see him and apologized. Tell him how much the dog means to you and assure him that nothing like this will ever happen again.'

'He wouldn't listen to me.'

'No game's lost till the final whistle,' said Mac firmly. 'It's worth a go.'

Gonk looked up at Mac with desperation. 'Will you come with me?'

Mac hesitated. Then he reached for his coat. 'Get in the car,' he said.

Mr Mills was gardening as Mac and Gonk got out of the car and walked cautiously up his front path.

'Mr Mills –'

'What do you want?' He looked up, leaning irritably on a spade.

'About the dog,' said Mac.

'The matter is in the hands of the police.'

'Aye. I know. But this lad has something to say to you.'

Gonk cleared his throat and Mr Mills looked at him with considerable hostility.

'I'm dead sorry about what happened, Mr Mills,' said Gonk in a rush. 'It'll never happen again.'

But Mr Mills simply stared at him in stony silence.

'He's a guard dog, see,' stuttered Gonk. 'That's why he went for you. Trained to tackle anyone who breaks in.'

'All the more reason for you to keep him under control.'

'We can assure you he will be in future, Mr Mills,' said Mac.

'So?'

'We're hoping that, in the face of this, you might want to withdraw your complaint.'

'Out of the question.'

Gonk came in desperately. 'But Mr Mills, Barney could be put down if the case gets to court.'

'Why – has he bitten someone before?'

Both Mac and Gonk were silent.

'He has, hasn't he?' said Mr Mills.

'Apparently,' replied Mac.

'I'm not surprised.'

'Please, Mr Mills,' Gonk's voice was trembling. 'He's a good dog. Dead soft when you get to know him.'

'Look, I'm sorry. There's really nothing I can do.'

'You mean there's nothing you *will* do.' The hostility surged in Mac's voice.

'No. I don't mean that. I mean there's nothing I *can* do about it. I'm a J.P. and I know a bit about the law. Once a complaint's been laid there's no way it can be withdrawn. The matter's out of our hands now and the law has to take its course.'

Mr Mills looked at them both and then turned abruptly away. 'I'm afraid that's it,' he said, walking into the house.

Gonk looked at Mac in despair. 'I told you he wouldn't listen!' he yelled. 'I told you.'

Looking as if he were going to cry, Gonk ran back to the car. Slowly and grimly, Mac followed him.

Rasputin was not an unkind man, but where money was concerned he had learnt to be hard for his own survival. So when he discovered from his solicitor that if Barney disappeared now court proceedings would be dropped, he began to have an idea that at first shocked even him. But as the idea gathered weight, Rasputin lost any thought of compassion and he sent Derek Cassidy round to the Junior Supporters' Club to retrieve Barney and have him put down.

Delighted at the opportunity to score off the gang who had always managed to better him, Cassidy went to the club-house only to discover that the dog was nowhere to be found. In fact Gonk had boarded Barney out with old Ted, the groundsman who was afraid of no one, and the gang had clubbed together to pay for Barney's keep.

Eventually Rasputin was forced to confront the gang in the Junior Supporters' Club, by which time he had worked himself into a tremendous rage.

'Listen, you lot,' Rasputin snarled. 'Gimme that dog.' His mood was not helped by his solicitor's latest interpretation of the situation. In a few words he had told Rasputin that if the dog were not found, he might be fined at the rate of a couple of pounds a day – for ever.

Furiously, Rasputin grabbed Gonk and shouted, 'If anyone knows where the pooch is you do.'

'Sorry.'

'Look, son, it's not Derek Cassidy you're dealing with – it's me. And I don't play games. Where's the dog?'

'To have him put down, right?' shouted Gonk angrily.

'What I do with him has nothing to do with you.'

'Hasn't it?'

'Where is he?'

'I'm not saying.'

Realizing that he was wasting his time, Rasputin let Gonk go and rounded on the others. 'Well?'

There was total silence.

'O.K. This club is closed. As from now.'

'That's not fair,' said Becky, who was one of the gang now.

'Life gets harder, sweetheart.'

Rasputin walked out and the kids looked at each other hopelessly.

'Now what?' asked Gerry.

'Now we dig in,' said Gonk. 'No way does he get to Barney, whatever it costs us.'

'Don't you think you're being a bit heavy-handed – closing their club like that? Just because one of the kids is holding out on you.'

Mac and Elaine were in the office, trying to reason with Rasputin. But it was not an easy task.

'Look – every kid in the club knows where that dog is. They're just not saying.'

'If we kick the kids out,' said Mac evenly, 'we'll have the same problems as before. Vandalism –'

'So we get ourselves another couple of guard dogs,' interrupted Rasputin. 'Dogs that don't become pets.'

'I just can't believe that you're really prepared to put that dog down before the case comes up in court.'

'Look,' said Rasputin with seemingly superhuman patience. 'Suppose it *does* come up in court, and they say the dog's got to be put down. Do you think that for one moment the kids are going to give him up? Which still means I'll be forking out two quid a day for a dog I haven't even got.'

Elaine stared back at him.

'So forget it,' said Rasputin.

'Give it back,' said Mac. He waited for a reaction from the gang and there was none. 'If you don't it'll mean the police.'

Still there was silence.

'I tell you,' said Mac. 'He's dead serious.' He turned and walked over to the door. 'All right. Rasputin wants all your stuff out of here. Today.'

Once he had gone, Gonk turned to the others. 'So the police come. They can't prove we know where Barney is.'

'We wouldn't half be in trouble if they could,' said Gerry.

'We can't crack now,' replied Gonk in desperation.

'We're not cracking,' said Boxer.

'We're getting near it,' stated Gerry gloomily. 'We'd better start clearing up.'

Cassidy came into Mac's office in search of a screwdriver, just as Mac and Elaine were debating the issue of Barney.

'Try Ted,' said Mac wearily. 'He's got a shed full of screwdrivers.'

'By the way,' said Cassidy, arriving at the real reason for his visit. 'As manager I'm sure you'll be interested to know that there's no real need to be worried about the demise of the Junior Supporters' Club.' He looked delighted.

'I wasn't planning to lose any sleep over it.'

'You see – my own committee are more than willing to step into the breach and form their own junior section.'

'How nice.'

'I thought you'd be pleased.'

'There's just one question, Derek.'

'Yes?'

'You will make sure there's a blood test before any kid is admitted for membership.'

Cassidy leered at him in a semblance of a smile. 'You will

have your little joke, Mac.' He went out, the smile fixed on his face.

'Creep,' muttered Elaine.

To his delight, Cassidy found a tin of dog food in old Ted's tool shed during his hunt for a screwdriver. He went straight to Rasputin in Outer Space, who was studying a roll of figures he had just taken from the till. Both men were quite unaware that Gerry was emptying a machine near by.

'I've got a clue,' said Cassidy excitedly.

'What are you on about?' snapped Rasputin.

'Old Ted.'

'What about him?'

'I never thought he was a dog lover.'

'He isn't.'

'Wouldn't have thought he ate dog food himself.'

'Dog food?'

'In his shed. On the table.'

'I see,' Rasputin was suddenly alert. 'Let's go and take a look at Ted's place, shall we?'

He walked rapidly towards the door while Cassidy looked after him grinning, before following him out. Neither of them saw Gerry stealing towards the side exit.

They were too late. As Gerry and Gonk ran up towards old Ted's terraced house, Rasputin's Rolls pulled away. In the back they saw Derek Cassidy crouched beside Barney. They stood on the pavement, horrified, watching the Rolls speed down the road. Then Ted came out. He was very angry.

'You and your damn dog,' he said, coming up to them.

'What's up?' asked Gerry.

'Thanks to him I just lost me blooming job.'

Old Ted stumped back to his house, leaving Gerry and Gonk staring after him in dismay. Now everything had gone wrong.

Mac was not to escape gang pressure, and this time it was Jenny who was at him.

'You've got to have a word with Rasputin, Mac,' she declared. 'I mean – if that dog is put down I don't know what Gonk'll do.'

'Look,' began Mac feebly, 'he's just a dog.'

'No, he's not,' said Jenny with withering contempt. 'He's the club mascot. *Your* club's mascot. And you're not going to just stand by and watch him destroyed. Are you?'

Mac sighed. 'I'll go and see him,' he said wearily.

Barney was tied up to the radiator in Rasputin's office. He looked particularly loving and docile when Mac walked in.

'You can't be serious,' began Mac.

'What about?'

'Giving Ted the boot.'

'Why not?'

'Because he's the best groundsman in the business. That's why.'

'He helped those kids hijack the dog.'

'He felt sorry for them.'

'And he's lucky he's not facing charges. We can always find another groundsman.'

'If you think good ones are easy to find then you don't know much about football pitches.'

'He's fired and that's it.'

'So who's gonna cut the grass now?'

'You're always tellin' me you're the one who's paid to run things round 'ere.'

'I'm paid to run a football team, not prepare the pitch.'

'So find a replacement. There are three million on the dole – one of them must be a groundsman.'

'And the dog?'

'What about him?'

'You doing the job personally? Standing there while he's injected?'

'You think I haven't got the bottle?'

'Have you?'

Rasputin got up, untied the dog and led him out of his office. Mac watched him go, suddenly afraid.

Rasputin pulled his Rolls to a gliding halt outside the vet's and Barney looked up at him lovingly, trying to nuzzle at his face. Rasputin looked down at him, swallowed, went to open the door, swallowed again and stared back into Barney's eyes.

When Derek Cassidy came into Rasputin's office, he saw Barney chained to the radiator.

'Yes?' asked Rasputin irritably.

'Is there anything you wanted doing?' asked Cassidy, staring at Barney.

'Yes, get that flamin' dog something to eat.'

'But –'

'Do what I tell you.'

'Of course.'

Startled and flummoxed, Cassidy obeyed.

'Dad.'

'Mm.' Inspector Glossop wanted peace, not more desperate questions from Wurzel. Irritably, he put down his newspaper.

'There must be something you can do about Barney. Like getting the charges dropped.'

'No.'

'But –'

'I can't take advantage of my position. Just because my son's involved.'

Inspector Glossop picked the newspaper up again, conscious of his son's persistence.

'He was just being a good guard dog,' argued Wurzel.

'A guard dog?'

'Yes.'

'You never told me he was a guard dog.'

'Why? Does it make a difference?'

'It could do. Depends if there was a handler down at the ground.'

'Gonk mostly.'

'He can't be described as a proper handler. Are there notices down there warning people about a guard dog?'

'No.'

'Then that makes things worse.'

'Can they be?' asked Wurzel.

'Yes,' said Inspector Glossop, closing his eyes. 'They could be.'

When Rasputin came back from court, he marched straight into Mac's office.

'How did it go?' asked Mac.

'It didn't.'

'Why?'

'Case adjourned at the request of the police.'

'How come?'

Rasputin looked at him grimly. 'Apparently evidence has come to light that the whole thing is more serious than we thought. For me.'

'What evidence?'

'It seems one of your little friends has a dad who's a top cat at the nick.'

'That's Wurzel.'

'And little thicko Wurzel blabs to his dad that the dog is only doing what he's doing because he's a guard dog – a trained guard dog.'

'Well, he is,' said Mac defensively.

'Yes – and if you have a guard dog you have warning notices and a proper handler.'

'None of which we have.'

'Right, and thanks to thicko's big mouth I'm gonna get done for that as well.'

Matters had now become so serious that Elaine decided to take some independent and direct action. She went to see Mr Mills, sweating with anxiety as she rang his front door bell.

'Well?' He opened the door, cold and impassive.

'I'm Elaine Murphy. My husband –'

'I know who you are.'

'I've come about the dog,' she said flatly.

'Now look –'

'*Please* listen to me. I do appreciate how you must feel, but I wonder if you could just clear up one point for me.'

'Well?' He was still frosty.

'I've been talking to the two boys concerned about the incident, and they told me something they'd never mentioned before.'

'Oh?'

'They said it looked as if you were going to take a kick at the dog. Now, of course they could be lying to save the dog's life. They're both heartbroken and they blame themselves bitterly for what happened. If you tell me they're lying I'll naturally take your word on it.' She paused. 'Were they lying, Mr Mills?'

Mills paused in exasperation. But he was a basically honest man. 'The dog was growling at me.'

'But you did threaten to kick him.'

'I suppose so. Only to warn him off.'

'Did you tell the police that when you laid the complaint?' She was bolder now, more sure of herself.

Mills paused. Then he said, 'No, I didn't.'

'Don't you think you should have?' Elaine's voice shook.

'That dog's vicious,' Mills said.

'Only if he feels his friends are being threatened. Apart from that he's very gentle. Well, I must go. Thanks for telling me, and I'm sorry to have troubled you again. Goodbye.'

Elaine walked away down the garden path. Mills stood at the front door looking uneasy.

As Inspector Glossop came in he heard Gonk shouting at Wurzel in the front room.

'You've done all this. You threw a stick in the road and that started it. Then you blab to your old man. Without you none of this would have happened, would it? You're an idiot!'

'Oi,' said Inspector Glossop, but Gonk dashed past him and was out of the door in a few seconds.

'What was all that about?' he asked his disgruntled son.

'You.'

'Me?'

'Yeah, tellin' em down at the station that Barney was a guard dog.'

'As a station officer I can hardly ignore the fact – it's my patch the dog's on.'

'I told you as my dad, not as a copper.'

'You told me as a copper because you hoped you could use your dad.'

'Now all my mates reckon I'm a grass.'

Wurzel ran out of the room and upstairs to his bedroom, leaving his father staring thoughtfully after him.

'There's a Mr Mills to see you.'

'Oh yes.'

The desk sergeant paused. 'About the dog.'

'Yes.'

Inspector Glossop began to head for the interview room.

'Sir?'

'Mm?'

'You know, I was making inquiries about the dog. On the Q.T. Well, it turns out he attacked a teenager at a football match.'

'Why?'

'Apparently he provoked it. Our lads were sure the kid had been tormenting the dog. The kid and his mates had been in trouble with the police already that day and got slung off the ground. Seems the lad who got bitten swore the dog had gone for him and his mates backed him up. We'd no choice but to take their word for it.'

'I see. Right, I'll go and see Mills now.'

'Yes, sir. Thought that might help, sir.'

'It does.'

'Are you the senior officer in this station?'

'I am, sir.'

'Right.' Mills moved uncomfortably in his chair. The interview room was small, stuffy and squalid.

'I want to talk to you about this dog business. I want to withdraw my complaint.'

'I'm afraid it's a bit late for that, sir. The matter's already been laid before the court once.'

Mills cleared his throat. 'There's one aspect of the matter I should have made clear. Before.'

'Oh?'

'You see, it could be interpreted that I – er – I menaced the dog.'

'Could it, sir?'

'Would that make any difference to the case?'

'I think it might, sir.' Inspector Glossop picked up a large sheet of white paper. 'Would you care to expand?'

The waste ground at the back of the large, derelict factory was covered in scrubby grass and bushes. The grass was covered with old prams, redundant domestic equipment and the twisted frames of a number of bicycles. There were even a couple of rusted car chassis and some kids had built a camp out of broken boards and rotten mattresses in one of the dusty bushes. On the blank, scarred factory wall a set of goals had been chalked up and Gerry, the Prof and Boxer were taking shots at them. They were being watched by Jenny, Sheila and Becky. Suddenly Wurzel rushed up to them, looking wildly excited.

'Here's Mighty Mouse,' said Gerry with hostility.

'Where's Gonk?' asked Wurzel.

'We haven't seen him for a couple of days,' said Boxer hollowly. 'he won't come out. Just sits inside moping.'

'You'd be the last person he'd want to see anyway,' said Sheila, walking up.

'But I've got news for him,' said Wurzel triumphantly.

'What?' asked Gerry.

'Dad's just come home from work and says they're not proceedin' any further in the case. So Barney's in the clear.'

There was a noisy, spontaneous burst of applause and Wurzel basked in the unfamiliar glow of returning popularity.

'Does that mean we get the clubhouse back?' asked Becky.

'Well,' pondered Gerry. 'Rasputin would 'ave no reason for us not having it back, would he?'

'Let's go to Outer Space and see him,' said Jenny.

'And we'll pick Gonk up on the way,' said Boxer, 'and put him out of his misery.' He turned to Wurzel. 'By the way, Wurzel . . .' He advanced towards him threateningly and Wurzel backed off, looking worried. 'Well done,' said Boxer.

*

'It may be good news for you,' said Rasputin, 'but it doesn't solve my problem, does it? Thanks to you I'm clobbered for eight hundred quid.'

'But why?' asked Becky.

'Because the law still says I should have proper notices and a handler.'

'To be honest,' put in the Prof irritatingly, 'that's not exactly our mistake, is it?'

Rasputin glared at him. 'No, Einstein – it was my mistake. My second mistake, actually.'

'What was your first?' asked the Prof.

'Letting you lot in here in the first place,' growled Rasputin.

Boxer walked down the gloomy corridor of the old Roller Skating Rink with the rest of the gang. They were a miserable crew, all too conscious of the fact that, despite everything, they had still lost the most precious thing – their club-room.

Then Boxer gave a loud war-cry and turned to the others. 'I've got an idea!' he yelled, and raced back towards Rasputin's office.

'There's a bit of a deputation to see you, sir,' said the desk sergeant, coming into Inspector Glossop's office. He looked slightly agitated. 'And your son's one of 'em.'

Inspector Glossop groaned. 'Send them in,' he said.

Mac, Elaine, Rasputin and the gang came tumbling through the door and suddenly Inspector Glossop's quite large office seemed very small.

'What's all this?' asked Glossop.

'Well,' said Mac. 'There's been a bit of a development.'

'Oh?'

'The dog's not a guard dog. He's a club mascot.'

Glossop frowned and tried to avoid the piercing look in his son's eye. He turned to Rasputin.

'Did you or did you not buy that dog to guard your ground?'

'Yes, I did. And of course the minute I got him I had every intention of complying with all the requirements of the law in this matter. Being the good solid and upright citizen that I am.'

'Oh yes.'

'I always try –' continued Rasputin, but Glossop raised a hand.

'But you didn't fulfil the requirements of the law, did you, Mr Jones?'

Mac intervened. 'Because Barney was never used as a guard dog. As manager I wouldn't allow it.'

'He's so dominating,' intoned Rasputin.

'So we adopted him and turned him into the club mascot,' said Elaine.

'So you see, Dad,' Wurzel was unable to keep quiet any longer. 'There's no case to answer, is there?'

'Keep out of this,' snapped Glossop. 'It was you who started all this.'

'Sorry, Dad.'

'But he does have a point,' said Mac. 'There *is* no case to answer. Not now.'

'My legal adviser assures me that if the case does come to court, this new evidence will kill it. You won't have a snowball's chance in hell of making it stick.'

'Very neat,' said Glossop.

'And true?' asked Mac.

'And very true,' replied Glossop. 'Now why don't you all go and play somewhere else, and take my son with you.'

The Rolls glided up to the shabby door of Ted's terraced house. Rasputin got out and knocked at the tarnished paintwork. Ted opened the door. He looked beaten.

'Oh, it's you.'

'About that job.'

'What job?'

'It's still there if you want it.'

Ted looked at him as if he was mad. Then he said, 'I'll think about it, Mr Jones.'

Gonk and Wurzel rang the bell of Mr Mills' door. Eventually he opened it and looked out in surprise and mounting concern.

'Now what?' he asked.

'We just wanted to thank you,' said Gonk. 'For what you did for the dog.'

'Yeah,' chimed in Wurzel. 'Thanks.'

'Keep the animal under control in future, then,' retorted Mr Mills.

'We will,' said Gonk.

'And Mr Murphy has sent you these,' said Wurzel, holding out some bits of paper in a grubby hand. 'Two stand tickets for the next home match.'

'But I've never been to a football match in my life.'

'You're never too old to start,' said Wurzel, tactlessly.

'I'm not that old,' retorted Mills indignantly. Just then a dog began to bark from the house.

'And if you ever want me to take your dog for a walk —'

'I'll ask,' said Mills coolly as he began to close the door. 'Do thank Mr Murphy for me.' He closed the door.

Walking back down the garden path, Wurzel turned to Gonk and said, 'I get the feelin' he won't take me up on the offer of that walk.'

'So do I,' said Gonk.

Nobody ever really settled down to a quiet routine at Dunmore United. Mac was too busy building up the club's fortunes to mark time, Rasputin was as unpredictable as ever – and there was always the Junior Supporters' Club to make things hum.

But for once the new excitement came from outside, in the shape of Stevie King, a new player Mac had recruited for United. While Elaine was staying with her mother and the food in the Murphy household was subsequently deteriorating, Stevie burst in like a big handsome bombshell. He was in his late teens, with a friendly personality and a strong Liverpool accent. But the first question Boxer asked him had nothing to do with football.

'Can you cook?'

'Well, I can boil water.'

'Pity, because when it comes to home cookin', Mac makes a great football manager.'

Stevie King had been invited to stay until he found digs. But there were other requests that Mac soon voiced.

'We've got this penalty competition for kids and it's the final shoot-out tonight. Our regular goalie's hurt his back and I was going to step in but –'

'Count on me,' said Stevie.

Mac beamed at him and later said to Boxer, 'That lad's gonna fit in round here.'

'Nice guy,' said Boxer.

Mac gave him a friendly warning look. 'Keep him that way,' he said.

Sheila was Gerry's girl-friend and they were very fond of each other. So it was with considerable trepidation that she told him she had too much homework to watch him go through his paces at the penalty competition. Gerry went off in a sulk and Sheila regretfully began to get on with her homework. But the continuous arguing of her parents soon put a stop to that, and after a few minutes she decided to follow Gerry down to the United Ground. She slammed the door on her parents' quarrelling and ran off down the road. Sheila knew there would be a row later, but she didn't care. They were always quarrelling now. Her mother was exhausted and almost unable to cope, and she didn't give her husband a chance to help. In fact, it was rather as if she wanted him to annoy her so that she had an excuse to grumble at him continuously.

But once Sheila was on the touch-line she tried to forget the problems at home and watch Gerry trying to get his shots past the very agile Stevie King. But although Gerry's shots were very respectable he stood no chance. Neither did Boxer, and it was only Gonk who succeeded in getting past Stevie. There was tremendous applause while Rasputin hissed at Mac, 'That's three out of three that kid's hit. You do realize it's a sin he's not on our books.'

'You know he doesn't want to be a pro,' snapped Mac.

Rasputin scowled. He was used to getting what he wanted – and in Gonk's case he wasn't.

Rasputin then announced Gonk the winner and conspiratorially took him aside. Putting his arm round him in a fatherly way, Rasputin did his best.

'You see son, I know that when you were young and foolish last season you 'ad this 'ang up about bein' the next James Herriot. But now that you're older and wiser don't you think it's about time you reconsidered my offer of signin' for us?'

'I'm sorry, Mr Jones. I still want to be a vet.'

'You're crazy,' said Rasputin. 'Turning down an offer like this.'

'That's what all my mates tell me.'

'And they're right.'

'Maybe, but I still want to be a vet.'

Rasputin turned his back on him and stumped away. 'Be a flamin' vet,' he shouted. 'I hope you get foot and mouth!'

'Thanks,' said Gonk.

'My name's Sheila Fielding. I'm Chairperson of the Junior Supporters' Club.'

Stevie King leant against a goalpost and grinned. 'I'm the boy wonder,' he said.

'Have you got any pictures of yourself? We sell things like that in our shop on match days.'

'You'll have to take one specially.'

'We'll do that.'

'See you around.'

Stevie wandered off and Sheila watched him go. Gerry appeared.

'I thought you said you weren't comin' out.'

'Changed my mind, didn't I?'

'Somethin' the matter?'

'No. Why should there be?'

'You were scowling.'

'So – I was scowling. What's that to you?'

'All right, I only asked.'

'Who's that bloke over there? He's doing some scowling too.'

She was looking towards a big, sombre man in his thirties who was watching Stevie King walking off towards the changing rooms.

'That's Harry Bradshaw. He's been the United goalie for

years. Don't you know him? After all, you're Chairman of –'

'Of course I know him. He just looked different today, that's all.'

'Different?'

'He looked so angry. It made him look different.'

Mac came up the corridor just as Harry Bradshaw was looking at the team sheet on the notice board.

'So the kid stands in for me Saturday then?'

'You did say you'd hurt your back.'

'It's improving.'

'Too late,' said Mac abruptly. 'I've already told him he's playing.'

As Mac walked away, the frown increased on Harry's face.

'And where, might I ask, 'ave you been?'

Mrs Fielding was furious as she paced up and down the living room. Mr Fielding was sitting in a chair, trying to keep out of it, but knowing he couldn't.

'Down the club.'

'You went out when I told you to finish your homework?'

'I just had to get out for a bit, Mum.'

'Well?' Mrs Fielding turned to her husband and glared at him.

'Well?' he replied.

'Aren't *you* going to say anything?'

'I say – don't let's get this out of proportion, Dorothy.'

'I'm not getting anything out of proportion. I told her what I told her and she deliberately ignored me.'

Mr Fielding got wearily to his feet.

'And where are you going?'

'Out!'

'Typical – always running away from everything.'

He grabbed his coat and thrust open the door.

'Thanks for your continued support,' said Mrs Fielding with a cold, angry smile.

For reply Mr Fielding slammed the door, and Sheila bent her head over her schoolbooks.

'It's not fair,' said Mrs Fielding, close to tears. 'I get no support.'

'What do I get?' wondered Sheila.

Mac was winding up his pre-match pep talk to the team in the changing rooms. Among them was Stevie King.

'Now remember,' said Mac. 'They're faster than we are up-front. But they're also inclined to commit a lot of people forward. So we play it the way we've worked it this week. We wait. We stay patient. And if we can we hit 'em on the counter. Right?'

There were murmurs of assent from the team.

'Now their most dangerous player is that big target man of theirs, Morrison. If he gets any room to work at all, make no mistake about it, he'll crucify us. So it's up to you to close him down, Bill. Make him think by the end of the match that you and him are Siamese twins.'

'Right, Boss,' said Bill.

'Now, let's go to work.'

They all stood up and began to clatter out of the room.

'A wee word in your ear.'

'Yes, Boss?'

'Stay cool and stay awake out there. And no fancy stuff. I'm a big fan of Rudolf Nureyev but only when he's ballet dancing. O.K.?'

'O.K. Boss.'

'And good luck.'

'Thanks.'

Stevie looked a little nervous and Mac put a hand on his shoulder.

'You'll be all right, son,' he said.

Stevie King *was* all right. He played a terrific match and the gang cheered him till they were hoarse. His goalkeeping was magnificent, and in the second half of the game he went high for a dangerous cross ball and cleared it beautifully. But his clearance was picked up in mid-field by Morrison, the striker Mac had warned his team about. Morrison came storming through with the ball and as he crossed into the box, Bill lunged at him and brought him crashing down. The ref immediately pointed to the penalty spot and Morrison placed the ball so that he could take the kick himself. Stevie faced him tensely. Morrison came striding in, hit a tremendous shot – and Stevie saved it with an acrobatic dive.

It wasn't only the kids who went wild. Rasputin was on his feet cheering and even Mac was grinning. The only person who wasn't on his feet was Harry Bradshaw.

Later, Sheila called round at Mac's house so that she could show Stevie the proofs of the pictures they had had taken of him. Boxer and Stevie were just pushing away half-finished plates of a particularly evil steak and kidney pie that Mac had made, and the first comment Boxer made was 'You've come about the cook's job, have you?'

'You'll be lucky.'

'What's wrong with the cooking?' asked Mac threateningly.

'It's a real treat,' said Boxer. 'You never know what's going to turn up next.'

'What happens next,' said Mac slowly, 'is you're going to dry up.'

Reluctantly Boxer followed Mac into the kitchen, leaving Stevie with Sheila.

'Do you want to see these photos?' she asked. 'You ought to choose the ones we sell.'

Stevie looked through the proofs avidly.

'Not exactly Robert de Niro, am I?'

'I think you look great in all of them,' said Sheila enthusiastically.

'Which one do you think's the best then?'

'That's my favourite.'

'That's the one then.'

'Right.'

Stevie sat back in his chair.

'So you're the club Chairperson then?'

'That's it.'

'Not something we have a lot of up in Liverpool, chairpersons.' He smiled at her and Sheila found herself blushing. 'Mind you,' he continued, 'up home they still think women's rights is what they use to smack your face with when you've been cheeking 'em.'

They both laughed and Sheila said, 'When the photos are ready would you autograph some of 'em for us?'

'Sure.'

There was an awkward pause and Sheila felt herself beginning to blush again. Quickly she said, 'I'd better be going then.'

'See you.'

''Bye.'

Sheila stumbled to the door. When she had gone, Stevie stood for a moment thinking. Then he picked up some dirty plates and went out into the kitchen with them.

The next morning, Stevie King was training hard in the gym with the rest of the first team. He was just raising a real sweat when Mac and Rasputin walked in. Stevie stopped training and, breathing hard, looked at them quizzically. Mac soon enlightened him.

'I've just had a phone call about you.'

'Me?'

'Seems every goalie in the country's crippled and they want you for the Young England squad.'

'Me?' said Stevie again.

'Well, I said I couldn't play. And Rasputin here's too long in the tooth. They want you to play in their International next Wednesday night.'

'You're havin' me on.'

'I thought it was a joke myself, but apparently it's authentic. But who'd want to play for England anyway.'

Rasputin could bear it no longer. 'Don't take any notice of this big Scottish nit,' he said. 'Congratulations.'

'It's incredible.'

'In the meantime,' said Mac. 'Do carry on.'

'You bet.'

Stevie turned back to his training with twice the enthusiasm. As they walked back down the corridor Rasputin said to Mac. 'You know, if I didn't know you better I'd say you wasn't very glad about having a Young England International on the books.'

'I'm pleased for the kid,' said Mac. 'He deserves it. But I'm not that pleased for us.'

'Why?' said Rasputin impatiently.

'Mr Chairman – we're a Fourth Division club with a not very distinguished record for the past hundred years. Now suddenly we find ourselves with a player who's got what it takes to get to the top. I mean straight to the top. Now just wait for all those managers of all those big clubs to see him on Wednesday at Wembley. You won't have to wait very long to see their cheque books.'

'Over my dead body.'

'I hope so.'

'The trouble with you, Mac, is that you've got no faith.'

Rasputin ran up the stairs to his own office, leaving Mac with a troubled look.

Sheila and Gerry walked in to the Fieldings' front room in a state of considerable excitement.

'Dad,' Sheila burst out. 'Gerry says the kids down the club are gettin' a trip up to Wembley to see Stevie King play for Young England next Wednesday night. Is it O.K. if I go?'

'I don't see why not.'

But Mrs Fielding said agitatedly, 'Wembley? At night?'

'There's a gang of us goin', Mum.'

'How will you get there and back?'

'On the train,' said Gerry. 'A mini-bus would be too pricey.'

'That'll mean a late train home,' said Mrs Fielding.

'Not too late,' said Gerry. 'Ten – half past.'

'I'll be fine, Mum. Honest,' insisted Sheila.

'On a half-past ten train? Full of football hooligans?'

But Gerry had decided that things were getting too hot to stay. 'Anyway,' he muttered, 'I'll leave you all to sort it out. See you tomorrow, Sheel.'

Once he had gone Mr Fielding tried to back Sheila up.

'I still say if there's a few of them going, give it a swing.'

'And our daughter finds herself in the middle of a riot?'

'Come on, Mum,' said Sheila. 'It's only a Young England game.'

'At which they'll still have soccer hooligans.'

'You don't mind me going to United games.'

'United isn't Wembley. Or London at half past ten at night.'

It was then that Mr Fielding put his foot down. 'Tell them you're going.'

'But I don't want to go if Mum doesn't want me to.' Sheila was almost in tears.

But Mrs Fielding had had enough and she suddenly blazed out, 'Please go. I don't want anyone to take any notice of my feelings.' She ran out of the room and Sheila stared at her father in desperation.

'What's going wrong, Dad?'

'Listen,' he said quietly. 'Go to the match. I'll fix your mother.'

*

The heady atmosphere of Wembley had taken all the gang in its grip and as they queued at the turnstiles they were deliriously happy. The only member who was uneasy was Sheila. Her mother had hardly spoken to her since she had opposed the trip, and she had remained stonily at her ironing board instead of kissing Sheila goodbye. But Sheila didn't want to spoil the evening for the others and when she thought of Stevie and his great chance, she was able to put her mother and the troubled situation at home out of her mind. For a while.

'England. England.' The chant from the crowd roared through the night and the atmosphere was electric. Rasputin and Mac had also arrived and were sitting expectantly in their seats. Then the crowd went mad as the two teams marched out on to the pitch. A few minutes later the match was on – and Stevie was put through his paces. The English goal was attacked again and again – and Stevie's saves were brilliant. By half-time he had more than proved himself and Rasputin turned to Mac.

'Comin' to the bar for a quick one?'

'No, thanks.'

'You know, Mac, you're terrific company at a match.'

'It's my stomach muscles. They get all knotted up,' said Mac with a wry smile. 'Couldn't face anything.'

Rasputin grinned. 'I'm off to celebrate. We've got some kid there.'

'Right,' said Mac, as Rasputin pushed his way out through the thronging crowd.

'Mr Rasputin Jones?'

'Yeah.' Rasputin put down his pint on the corner of the bar. He looked up to see two very obviously American gentlemen. One of them, a large fleshy man, was in his fifties. He looked prosperous and tough.

'The name's Larson,' he said.

'Oh yeah?'

Next to him stood a swarthy, rugged-looking character in his late thirties.

'The name's Laski,' he said.

'So?' Rasputin looked at them suspiciously.

'We've got something in common,' said Larson.

'You two have?'

'Funny guy. No, you and me.'

'What's that?'

'We both own football clubs.'

'I see.'

Larson shot out a hand. 'The name's Wayne – and this is my manager Joe. We run the Diego Torpedoes.'

'That's nice for you.'

'We're enjoying the game,' said Laski.

'Especially your boy in goal,' said Larson.

'Yeah, he's good.'

'I want him,' said Larson.

'Then you're going to be disappointed, sunshine,' said Rasputin very sweetly. 'He's not for sale.'

'When I want something, Mr Jones, I always get it,' replied Larson softly.

'That's something else we have in common. So forget it.'

'Aren't you being a little hasty?'

'I have been known to be. Yeah.'

'Don't you even want to hear what I'm prepared to offer you for him?'

'No charge for listening, I suppose,' grinned Rasputin. Larson hesitated, and Rasputin wondered whether he knew that he had met his match at last.

After the match, the fans streamed away in vast hordes. It was on the steps that Gerry realized Sheila was no longer with them. Telling the others to carry on to the station, he hurried back to the emptying stand where he found Sheila, sitting alone.

'What are you doing here?' he asked urgently. 'You'll miss the train.'

'I don't want to catch it.'

'What are you on about?'

'Nothing. I don't want to catch the train.'

'What's up?'

'Trouble at home.'

'Oh. Well – everybody has rows. Mum and Dad are always on at each other. And what about you and me?'

'Not like the rows in my place. Something terrible's goin' to 'appen, Gerry. I know it.'

'You mean your folks might split up?'

'They might, and then what 'appens to me?'

'It'll blow over.'

'Will it? They've been at it for months.'

'But how's missin' the train goin' to 'elp? It'll only make things worse.'

Sheila looked up at him as she realized the truth of what he had said. Then an attendant clinched the matter.

'What's your game then?'

'Football,' said Gerry.

'Clear off – it's over.'

'All right, we're going.' Gerry took Sheila's hand. 'Come on – we might just make it,' he yelled as they began to run up the steps.

'That's done it.'

'Yeah.'

'Now it *is* worse.'

'Don't rub it in.' Sheila looked miserably at the barrier and the back end of the train as it disappeared out of the station.

'We'll just have to catch the next one,' she said, sitting down heavily on a porter's trolley. She felt exhausted.

'There's only one problem to that,' said Gerry.

'What's that?'

'There isn't one. That *was* the last train.'

'The train's probably late, that's all.'

Mr Fielding stared helplessly at his wife, while she returned his stare, tight-lipped and with that look in her eye that he knew meant 'I told you so'.

Meanwhile, Gerry and Sheila had been desperately trying to phone Mac's house, as neither of them was on the phone. Boxer had just rushed in from the match as the phone rang for the last time. He ran to pick it up but it was too late. They had given up. A few minutes later Mac and Stevie arrived. Boxer had made them coffee and as he handed Stevie a cup, he said, 'Great performance tonight, Stevie. Fantastic.'

'Do you really think so?' asked Mac.

'Take no notice of 'im,' said Boxer. 'You were great.'

'Thanks.'

'We 'ad a bit of a problem though.'

'Oh?' said Mac grimly.

'We lost Gerry and Sheila on the way 'ome.'

'How do you mean *lost* them?' sighed Mac.

'Well, Sheila 'ad been behavin' dead peculiar all night – hardly talkin' and that. Then after the game she stayed in the stand and Gerry went to keep her company. They missed the train.'

It was at that point that the telephone rang again, and Mac went to answer it. It was Gerry's voice crackling away at the other end.

'We missed the train.'

'So we hear. What do you want me to do about it?'

'We was wonderin' if Boxer could nip round to our place and Sheila's to tell 'em what's happened.'

'Give me your number and we'll call you back in a quarter of an hour,' said Mac wearily, scrabbling for a pen. 'And just tell me – when *isn't* there going to be a crisis with you lot?'

In the end, Mac decided to drive back to London to pick up Gerry and Sheila. It seemed the best thing to do, particularly as Mrs Fielding was still exuding vast disapproval, with dire predictions of what would happen to her daughter in the wicked city.

When he returned at two in the morning, with Sheila and Gerry safely in the back of the car, Mrs Fielding was in a highly agitated state. As Sheila stumbled sleepily through the door, Mrs Fielding said with great feeling, 'Thank God.'

'Sorry, Mum.'

'That's all right. As long as you're safe.'

Mr Fielding turned gratefully to Mac. 'I'm very grateful to you.'

'That's O.K.' Mac grinned. 'She's a good bairn.'

He went back to the bed that he had been longing for throughout the long journey.

'Have you had any supper, love?' asked Mrs Fielding.

'I don't want any, thanks. I just want to get to bed.'

'Off you go then.'

Sheila went into the hall and closed the door. But as she began to climb the stairs to bed, she heard her parents beginning to quarrel again and she paused with a feeling of depressing certainty.

'Go on,' Mr Fielding was saying. 'You told me so.'

'Do I need to say it again?'

'Anybody can miss a train. She came to no harm.'

'The point is she could have.'

'Look for –' Both her parents' voices were beginning to rise as Sheila hurried up the stairs. She clapped her hands over her ears and began to run.

*

10

Without doubt Derek Cassidy was United's snoop, and he was at it again as Mac came along the corridor in a track-suit, carrying a soccer ball. Waiting for Mac were the determined team of Larson and Laski, and Cassidy, pretending to study the notices on the board, paused to listen avidly.

'Mac Murphy?' drawled Larson.

'That's me.'

'We're looking for Rasputin Jones. It's about the deal we discussed last night.'

'Deal?'

'Yeah – we talked with him at Wembley Stadium about buying Stevie King from you.' Larson paused, and his buddy, Laski, took a shrewd, fleeting look at Mac's bewildered face.

'Didn't he tell you about it?'

'No.'

'Oh well. I guess he would have gotten round to it today sometime. Can you tell us where we might find him at the moment?' said Larson quickly.

'He has an office – at a place round the corner they call Outer Space.'

'Thanks.'

'But if I were you,' continued Mac. 'I'd leave it for a wee while yet. I shouldn't think he'll be there for at least another half an hour.'

'Thanks again.'

'You're welcome.'

Mac went straight into his office, slammed the door and threw the soccer ball down. He was furious. For a moment he stood there angrily. Then he hurried out.

As Larson and Laski were easing themselves into a large American car, Cassidy caught up with them breathlessly.

'Hey.'

'Yeah?' said Larson.

'The name's Cassidy. Derek Cassidy. I'm Chairman of the United Supporters' Club.'

'Yeah?' said Larson, completely unimpressed.

'I also work for Mr Jones at Outer Space.'

Larson shrugged and Cassidy hurried on.

'I couldn't help overhearing what Mr Murphy was saying. In fact Mr Jones should be in his office now.'

'Is that so?' Larson looked at Laski as if he could smell a rat.

'Someone using delaying tactics?' whispered Laski.

Larson turned back to Cassidy. 'Can you direct us to this Outer Space?

'By a fortunate coincidence,' smarmed Cassidy, 'I'm on my way there myself.'

But Mac had beaten the Americans to it and was locked in an eyeball to eyeball confrontation with Rasputin.

'Look – nothing's finalized yet.' Rasputin was shifty and defensive.

'I should damn well hope not. Before I'd even been consulted.'

'I tried to call you last night. But I gather you were pickin' those dopey kids up.'

'The Yank said you'd discussed it at half-time. Yes or no?'

'Yeah.'

'I was sitting next to you all the way through the second half. Why didn't you tell me?'

'I wanted to think it out.'

'What is there to think about? We'd be crazy to sell him.'

'You sure? Do you know his market value?'

'I've never thought about it, since I had no plans for putting him on the market.'

'He's worth three hundred thousand quid.' Mac whistled. 'Yeah – three hundred thousand. Now I gather we could just do with that.'

'No. How the hell can I get a team together to get us up into the Third Division when every time we find ourselves a player we flog him?'

'I said I was thinkin' about it.'

'You'd better think very carefully, Mr Chairman. Because what you decide could have a very serious effect on our future relationship.'

Rasputin looked at Mac furiously and rasped out, 'One of these days you're gonna play that card once too often.'

There was a knock on the door and Rasputin yelled out, 'Who is it?'

Cassidy put his head through the door ingratiatingly. 'A couple of American gentlemen to see you, Mr Jones.'

Larson and Laski came in and Mac rose to his feet.

'I'll see you later,' he hurled at Rasputin.

'So you *did* get in early, Mr Jones,' said Larson.

'What do you mean?'

'Nothing. Now, what about this decision?'

'You'll have to wait.'

'I thought you were a man who could make decisions, Mr Jones. You disappoint me.'

'This time things aren't that simple.'

'How long?'

'I'll be in touch. I'll call your hotel.'

'Don't leave it too long. We fly back in two days. And by

then I'll want to know one way or the other or you can forget it.'

Larson and Laski turned to the door.

'We'll be hearing from you, I'm sure,' said Laski.

In the club-house, the gang were discussing the matter excitedly.

'Mac wouldn't really sell him, would he? He's the first decent player we've had since Jock,' said Jenny.

'And what a rat Jock turned out to be,' spluttered Wurzel, angry at the memory.

'Mac doesn't want to sell Stevie,' said Boxer. 'It's Rasputin who's after the loot as usual.'

'It would be terrible to lose him,' moaned Gerry. 'Just when we're candidates for promotion at last.'

Just then Gonk came rushing in to say that Stevie had a snazzy new car parked outside, and the boys pounded out. En route, Gerry said to Sheila, who was just arriving, 'What did your mum and dad say?'

'Nothin'.'

'Lucky you. I got it in the neck. See you in a minute.'

'O.K.'

Sheila took off her coat and sat down heavily. Becky, coming from behind the bar, immediately said, 'What's the matter?'

'I don't know what to do.'

'What about?'

'Everything's going wrong.'

'Tell me about it,' Becky said softly while Sheila rummaged in her bag.

'Look at this.'

'What is it?'

'My school progress report. It's awful.'

Becky glanced at it. 'We all get bad ones sometimes.'

'But it's all the time now. For the last few months I've not dared show Dad and Mum any of the reports.'

'How do you get away with it?'

'I forged Dad's signature.'

'You didn't!'

'I did! I can't concentrate because I'm worrying all the time.'

'Worrying? What about?'

'Mum and Dad. They're so uptight with each other all the time. Just one row after the other. I'm sure they're goin' to split up.'

'Oh, Sheel . . .' Becky came over and put her arm around Sheila's shoulders. 'I'm so sorry.'

Gently, Sheila began to cry.

Gonk, Boxer, Wurzel and Gerry were admiring Stevie's nifty new sports car.

'It's only secondhand,' Stevie was explaining, 'but it'll do a bit.'

'Does this mean you're stoppin'?'

'Stoppin'?' Stevie looked surprised. 'What do you mean?'

'Shut up, Wurzel!' hissed Boxer, but it was too late.

'I've only just got here,' said Stevie.

'I just heard a rumour, that's all,' said Wurzel, catching Boxer's agonized eye. 'A rumour that you might be goin' to America.'

Boxer groaned – as usual Wurzel was making matters worse.

'America?' Stevie looked dazed. 'Where did you hear that?'

Wurzel shrugged. 'Just a rumour among the other kids.'

'You lot?' Stevie looked hard at Boxer.

'It was somethin' we heard,' said Boxer. 'There's nothin' in it – just a buzz.'

Stevie looked at Boxer thoughtfully for a moment. 'Just a buzz, eh?' Then he got out of the car and began to walk towards the club offices. 'See you,' he said.

When Stevie was out of earshot, they all turned on Wurzel.

'You idiot,' said Boxer. 'You great, ravin' idiot.'

Mac was working out alone in the gym when Stevie came up to him.

'Is it true, Boss?'

Mac stopped and looked him up and down. 'Aye – it's true.'

'Couldn't somebody have told me?'

'Why?'

'It's my career for God's sake.'

'It hasn't got to that stage.'

'What stage *has* it got to?'

'They want you. But we aren't prepared to sell. At least I'm not.'

'And I hear it from a kid.'

'Which kid?'

'Boxer and the rest of the gang. I felt a right mug.'

'I'm sorry about that.'

'Well, do keep me informed, won't you? You know, give me a shout if the Russians come in on the act.'

And with that Stevie King strode angrily out of the gym.

Mac confronted Boxer a few minutes later and the rest of the gang waited in the club-house, anxious to see his wounds. Eventually he came in, looking considerably chastened.

'Rough?' asked Gonk.

'Put it this way,' replied Boxer. 'I think I know what the team feels like when they're two down at half-time – and Uncle Mac goes into the dressing room to tell them what he thinks.'

'What did he say?' asked Wurzel guiltily.

'Everything,' said Boxer.

Larson and Laski were tucking into two enormous steaks in a restaurant in the centre of the town when Rasputin rang. The waiter brought a telephone to the table and Rasputin told them, while the steaks were cooling, that Stevie was not for sale. When he had rung off, Larson pushed his plate away, took a long sip of bourbon and said, 'There's no such word as no in my vocabulary.'

'So?'

'We need to get at the kid ourselves.'

'Jones won't like that,' said Laski.

'Jones needn't know. We need to know where the kid lives. Now how do we do that?'

They thought for a few seconds. Then Larson said gleefully, 'Got it. That creep who runs the Outer Space dump.'

'Cassidy?'

'That's the guy.' He looked at his watch. 'They may still be open. Get hold of him for me – and make sure Jones doesn't get wise.'

'Now?' said Laski, looking sadly at his unfinished steak.

'Now,' said Larson firmly.

Outer Space was empty and Gerry was switching off the machines for the night. With him was Sheila.

'So what are you gonna do?'

'Forge Dad's sig – as usual.'

'You're crazy,' said Gerry. 'You can't get away with it for ever.'

'I've already done it, haven't I?'

'Go and tell your parents now. Get it over with.'

'No.'

'But why not?'

'Because I'll cause another row.'

Cassidy came bustling up. 'Get on with it now, Gerry. You're not paid to gossip.'

Gerry turned to Sheila. 'See you later then.'

'O.K.'

She went, slowly and apathetically. Gerry continued switching off the machines, worrying about her as he worked.

Then Cassidy turned round and saw Laski.

'Hallo.'

'How are you?'

'Overworked and underpaid.'

'Mr Larson was grateful for your help this morning.'

'It was a pleasure.'

'He wonders if you could help us again. For a small fee?'

'Well . . .' said Cassidy. 'I might be able to oblige.'

Next day Mac was taking a training session on the United pitch. He was a hard task-master, and there was no let up for the players as he put them through their exercise routine.

'All right,' he yelled at them. 'Come on – move it! We've got the first round of the League Cup on Saturday, so pull your fingers out.'

Eventually, sweating and tired, the players pounded back down the tunnel towards the dressing rooms. As Stevie came past, Cassidy was lying in wait for him.

'Stevie.'

Stevie paused, bewildered. He didn't know Cassidy and didn't really want to pause for introductions. He was exhausted, and still angry that no one had told him or consulted him about the American offer.

'You won't know me but I'm Derek Cassidy, Chairman of the Supporters' Club.'

'Hi.'

'An American gentleman asked me to give you this. It might be an idea if you exercised a certain amount of discretion in reading it. Yes?'

'I don't know what –'

But Cassidy had pressed the note into Stevie's hand and hurried on. Then Mac came up and Stevie hastily stuffed the note into his pocket.

'I'd like a word.'

'Sure, Boss.'

Mac led him towards the office and opened the door.

'Sit down.'

Stevie did as he was told.

'The Chairman's told the Yanks there's no deal. O.K.?'

Stevie shook his head slowly. 'O.K.'

'Now I want to tell you something important, son. It's my honest opinion as manager that you've got what it takes to go all the way to the top – once you've properly learnt your trade as goalkeeper. And you won't do that playing for a gimmick team in San Diego. Later on, someone's bound to make an offer we can't refuse and we'll have to let you go. But I expect you to stay with us at least till we've won ourselves promotion next season. Do I have your word on that?'

'Well –'

'O.K. I just expect it of you. Right?'

'Right, Boss.'

'Now go and have your shower.'

Slowly Stevie got up and went out, leaving Mac staring thoughtfully after him.

Once Stevie was outside in the corridor, he pulled the letter out of his pocket and began to read the contents intently.

Sheila was sitting doing her homework when her mother came in, carrying a basket of groceries. Her father was already in the room, buried in his paper.

As Mrs Fielding set down her groceries, she said, 'Janet Baldwin is in your class at school, isn't she?'

'Course.' Sheila was not really listening, concentrating instead on her maths.

'She wanted to know if we were going to the Parents' Evening tonight. I told her that you hadn't brought us a note.'

Sensing trouble, Sheila began to scheme. 'I never got one,' she said.

'How peculiar.'

'Yes.'

Then Mrs Fielding said something that electrified her. 'We'd better get ready then – or we'll be late.'

'It's just a Parents' Evening, Mum,' said Sheila persuasively. 'You've always said they were a dead waste of time.'

'That's not the point, dear.'

Suddenly Mr Fielding piped up. 'We want to know how you're doing, specially with your O levels coming up. I'll nip up and have a quick shave.'

'And I'll go and change,' said Mrs Fielding.

They both went out and Sheila buried her head in her hands. This was it.

Larson and Laski were where they both loved to be – in the middle of yet another expensive meal – when Stevie arrived at their table.

'Mr Larson?'

Larson grinned up at him. 'So you got my note.'

'I just came to see what it was all about. That's all.'

'You'd be a fool if you didn't. Pull up a chair.'

Stevie did as he was told and sat uncomfortably on the edge.

'Now,' said Larson, 'about your future – your future in Diego.'

'Mac Murphy thinks I'd learn more staying in the English game.'

'In the English Fourth Division? Or the Third if you're lucky. Don't give me that stuff. We've got some class players in the Torpedoes.'

'I promised Mac I'd stay with United – at least till we get in the Third Division.'

'He had no right to extract a promise like that from you,' snapped Larson. 'He was taking advantage of you.' He smiled. 'In this life you've got to look after yourself, boy – no one else will. And if you're a professional footballer you don't have too much time.'

'Rasputin wasn't prepared to sell me,' protested Stevie.

'Only when Murphy talked him out of it. He was ready enough at Wembley. In fact the guy reckoned that it was wrong to stand in the way of your career.'

'But if he still says no it's the end of it, isn't it?'

'It needn't be.'

'How come?'

'Who wants a discontented player?'

'But –'

'So get discontented if they're holding you against your will.'

Laski chimed in. 'What have you got to lose?'

'In the States you could be a star, and a millionaire,' continued Larson.

'I don't know –'

'Consider yourself. That's what Murphy's doing.'

'I'll sleep on it.'

'Do that. And if anyone asks about this conversation it didn't happen. Right?'

'Right.'

'Goodnight, Stevie. Sleep well.'

Stevie walked slowly away from the table.

'Brandy,' said Larson to the waiter. When it had arrived, Larson raised his glass to Laski.

'Let's drink to it.'

'It?'

'Success,' he said.

*

Sheila suddenly knew what she had to do. Hurriedly tearing a leaf out of her exercise book, she scribbled 'TO MUM AND DAD – SORRY – I CAN'T TAKE IT ANY LONGER.' She then crept upstairs, threw a few things in her suitcase, came down again, and hurried out of the door. A few moments later she was standing by the bus-stop, a sad, isolated figure.

Minutes passed and no bus came. Then a bunch of leather boys walked down the road, and seeing her, paused. For a while she tried to ignore them. Then one of them said, 'Goin' on your holidays, darlin'?'

Sheila started to shake with fear.

Stevie King walked slowly and thoughtfully out of the hotel, very tempted by Larson's offer, and at the same time, desperately worried that he was being disloyal to Mac. He knew that the right thing to do would be to stay and slog it out with United, to gain experience as a goalie and to push them through into the Third Division. Yet the Diego offer was so marvellous. He could be a star not an anonymous player in Dunmore. Also he would be rich, and he was certainly not rich now.

Then he saw the young girl at the bus-stop, trying to stop her suitcase being thrown about by a couple of yobbos. Stevie hesitated – and then he recognized the girl. It was Sheila. All thought of Larson and the Torpedoes and of Mac and United disappeared from Stevie's mind as he hurtled across the road.

'Oi,' he shouted.

The two young thugs looked up, saw him coming, panicked, and threw the suitcase at him. Dodging it, Stevie saw them split up. He also saw Sheila, crying, frightened, standing alone in the darkness. His temper rose and he gave chase to one of the yobbos, who immediately headed for a wall which overhung a street on a lower level. The boy cleared the wall, with Stevie a few inches away from him.

He landed like a cat and ran off, but Stevie misjudged his footing and fell on to the pavement with a cry of agony.

In a few seconds Sheila was kneeling beside him, as Stevie lay doubled up in pain.

'What's the matter?'

But Stevie only groaned. His face was very white and there were beads of perspiration on his forehead.

'What's the *matter*?' Sheila repeated the words, terrified at the look of him.

'Get an ambulance.'

'Yes – I –'

'Quick – it's my leg.'

With a sob, Sheila darted off into the night.

'I've phoned the police,' said Mr Fielding, still holding Sheila's letter in his hand.

'What'll they do?' asked his wife helplessly. Her eyes were red-rimmed from crying.

'They'll put out a description. And check bus stations and trains. What else can they do?'

'I can't believe she'd do this to us!'

'Or are we doing it to her?' he said quietly.

She stared up at him uncomprehendingly. 'What do you mean?'

'Think about it, love,' he returned grimly. 'Just think about it.'

'Where's Mac?' asked Sheila as she sat in the hospital corridor with Boxer.

'With Stevie.'

'It's all my fault.'

'Why? You got the ambulance, didn't you?'

'If I hadn't been there – it wouldn't have happened.'

'Why *were* you there?'

'I was runnin' away.'

'Where were you going?'

'Just going.'

'That's stupid.'

'Is it? With my parents at each other's throats all the time? Where else could I go? Besides – they were goin' to find out.'

'Find out what?'

'I've been forgin' my Dad's sig on my report cards so he wouldn't see how lousy they were.'

'That's stupid.'

'Can't you say anything else?'

Then Mac appeared.

'How is he?' asked Sheila, her voice quavering.

'He's O.K. for a guy with a broken leg.'

'Oh God.' Sheila was crying.

'It's a clean break – it could have been worse. Let's get you home.'

'NO!'

'What?'

'I don't want to go home.'

It was at this point that Mac lost his temper. 'Now look here, young lady. I don't know what you were doing at that bus-stop and I don't want to know. But I do know one thing – you're going home.'

'No.'

'Get in the car!'

'Come on,' said Boxer. 'Do what Mac says.'

Suddenly all the fight went out of Sheila. She was like a collapsed doll, and she allowed Boxer to lead her down the hospital corridor to the car park. She was going home.

The next morning Larson, tucking into bacon and eggs, was reading the sports page headline. 'YOUNG ENGLAND STAR'S UNLUCKY BREAK'. Beside him Laski munched toast mournfully.

'It could have been worse,' said Larson, laying down the paper.

'How?'

'He could have been on our books, instead of United's.'

'Yea. Guess so.'

'When's the flight?'

'I got one this afternoon.'

'Great.'

Larson was about to return to his breakfast when he was interrupted by the appearance of Derek Cassidy.

'What can I do for you?' asked Larson brusquely.

'You've heard the sad news about King?'

'Sure. It's a pity – we could have used the kid.'

'You're no longer interested?'

'There's nothing more useless than a goalie with a broken leg, Cassidy.'

'Where does that leave us?' asked Cassidy demurely.

'Nowhere, if you mean what's still in it for you. There's no deal, Cassidy.'

'It's no fault of mine.'

'Nor mine. Some you win. Some you lose.'

'So I get nothing.'

'You get nothing.'

Cassidy turned away. 'Thank you,' he said.

'Thank *you*,' said Larson with a grin. Derek Cassidy walked out in injured dignity and Larson lit a cigar.

'Creep,' he said. Then he turned to Laski.

'Tell me about the Italian kid you heard about,' he said.

Sheila was in a bad state. She wouldn't eat, had difficulty in sleeping, and was terrified that her deceit would be the last straw in the breaking up of her parents' marriage. So it was with considerable disquiet that she heard the knock on the door and saw her mother coming into her bedroom.

'Are you all right?'

'I'm fine.'

'You haven't touched your tea.'

'I'm not hungry, Mum.'

'Would you like some sandwiches?'

'No, thanks.'

'A glass of milk?'

'I'm not hungry, Mum. Don't worry about me.'

'But I do. We both do.'

There was a long silence. Then Mrs Fielding said, 'I know – I know how things have been in the past few months.'

'I don't know what you're talking about.'

'I think you do, love. Between your dad and me.'

'I –'

'You see, these things happen. You don't even know why sometimes. People just grow away from each other. They start to get on each other's nerves and it goes on from there. Do you understand?'

Sheila hesitated. Then she said, 'I think so.'

'But what I came to say was that your dad and I have talked. And we're both going to try to get on better with each other. Now I'm not going to say it's going to work out, but at least we're going to try.'

'Mum –' Sheila threw her arms around her mother.

'I'm sorry,' said Mrs Fielding.

'It's me who should be sorry,' replied Sheila.

'But you must promise me you'll never do that again, will you? At least not before coming to us – however bad things get.'

'I'll come to you, Mum,' said Sheila. 'I'll come to you.'

They held each other closely, suddenly knowing how much they loved each other.

Mac was sitting by Stevie's bedside. Stevie was sitting up and looking much better.

'The doctor says I can come home tomorrow.'

'Anything you need?'

'I'd be glad if you'd pick up my car for me.' He gave Mac his car keys which were on top of the locker.

'Where is it?'

'In the car park of the Claringdon Hotel.'

'The Claringdon? That's where the Yanks were staying.' He looked at Stevie challengingly. In fact Mac knew from Sheila that Stevie had gone to the Claringdon, but he was determined to play him for a little. Stevie stared back at him guiltily.

'They sent me a note.'

'Oh yes.'

'To come round for a chat. That was all.'

'Funny. I can't remember you mentioning it.'

'I was just curious to see what they were offerin', Boss. After all, you never did tell me.'

Then Mac suddenly turned hard. 'You do realize that meeting constituted an illegal approach to a player, to which you were a party?'

For a moment Stevie wondered if he should fight him. Then he decided against it.

'Sorry, Boss.'

'You sure as hell are now.'

'I wouldn't have agreed to anything behind your back.'

'You wouldn't have been in a position to, son, believe me.'

'I said I was sorry.'

Mac stared at him, still angry.

'Do you want your grapes back?' asked Stevie.

'Do you know what's the worst thing about being a football manager?' asked Mac slowly.

'What?'

'Having to manage footballers.'

11

Sheila was reluctant to go along to the club-house that week. Although her parents' quarrelling seemed to have stopped, she was still not sure how permanent the situation was. Also, she felt desperately guilty about Stevie and was still blaming herself for the accident. As a result Sheila just couldn't face the others. The gang were concerned about this, and Becky in particular was anxious to think of some way of leading Sheila back into the fold.

Mac, meanwhile, was forced to put Harry Bradshaw back in goal. Bradshaw took his re-inclusion with a sneer and a strange little smile. Then Mac interviewed Cassidy, told him that he'd been involved in an illegal approach to a player, and warned him that if anything of the kind happened again he would boot him out of the club. Once Cassidy had disappeared in a panic, Mac sat at the typewriter and began to pound at it, imagining the keys were Derek Cassidy's face. Time after time Cassidy had caused trouble, but Mac knew that he couldn't get rid of him until Rasputin was personally affected. But the time would come, he hoped. As Mac pounded the typewriter, there was a knock at the door and a pretty teenager walked in.

'You're Mac Murphy, aren't you?' Her accent was Liverpudlian and she had a disturbingly direct manner.

'That's me.'

'I'm Katie King – Stevie's big sister.'

'I didn't know he had a big sister.'

'Why should you? I just got back from abroad and I heard he'd been injured. So I came.'

'I see.'

'Can you tell me which hospital he's in?'

'He's due out today.'

'Where will he go?'

'He's staying at my place.'

'In that case, my deepest sympathies.'

'What do you mean?'

'You could be lumbered with him for the rest of your natural. Stevie's a great goalkeeper but when it comes to practical things like somewhere to live, he's a right wally.'

'I see.'

'When is he due back?'

'Two.'

'So if you give me the address I'll come and sort him out.'

'Certainly.'

Mac began to type the address.

'You're not very good at that, are you?'

'Can *you* do any better?'

'I can do sixty words a minute – with certificates to prove it.'

Mac looked up at her and grinned. Then he gave her the address.

'See you then.'

'I'll look forward to it.'

Katie hurried out of the office and Mac leant back, feeling exhausted. He wondered if everyone felt like that after a visit from Katie King.

Katie did more than sort out her brother Stevie. She sorted them all out by preparing Mac, Stevie and Boxer a huge and well-cooked meal. In the middle of all this, Elaine phoned to say that she would have to spend at least two more weeks looking after her mother. Glumly, Mac returned to the dining room to discover that the dynamic Katie had already found Stevie a flat.

Meanwhile, Boxer had invited Stevie to a party at the club-house and, with an eye to involving Sheila, Gerry went round to see her. A long battle ensued and eventually Gerry said in desperation, 'After all you are Chairperson and you owe it to him.'

'I'll think about it,' Sheila had said, but Gerry knew he had won.

Eventually, everyone attended the party in the club-house. Even old Ted was there, although Cassidy, of course, had not been invited. Sheila came and although very hesitant, she suddenly made a speech that moved them all.

'Speaking for myself – I was dead grateful for what Stevie King did for me the other night and I'm sorry that it cost him so much. As your Chairperson I'd like to ask him to agree to accept honorary life membership of the United Junior Supporters' Club.'

'A fate worse than death,' shouted Mac.

'And we'd also like him to accept this picture of the blindin' save he made for Young England at Wembley last week. Stevie – thanks a lot.'

There was a tremendous celebration and Stevie was obviously deeply touched.

There was also a surprise in store for Katie, for Mac asked her, in Elaine's absence, to come into the office and do some typing. At the end of the party, Boxer grinned at Mac and said, 'Looks like everything's turned out well.'

'With a broken leg? It's great for the team.'

'You know what I mean.'

Mac gave him a playful punch. 'Yeah – I reckon I know what you mean. For once.'

But, as ever, the fortunes of United were inevitably erratic, and on the day of the cup tie Harry Bradshaw did not arrive to play in goal. Frantic telephone calls by Mac revealed nothing, and eventually Mac sent Boxer over to Bradshaw's home on the estate. Boxer swooped off on his bike, and to his amazement found Harry washing his car. Boxer dismounted, unable to believe his eyes.

'Mac sent me,' he stuttered.

'Yeah?'

'He wants to know where you are.'

'That's obvious, son. I'm here.'

'But you should be at the match,' Boxer babbled.

'Now how can I be at the match if I'm here?'

'But you're playing today.'

'Am I?'

'Yeah.'

'Who says?'

'I do.'

'Oh my Gawd.'

Boxer passed the queuing fans, desperately pedalling his bike. He jumped off it and dashed into Mac's office, breathing heavily.

'Well,' said Mac. 'Is he there?'

'He's there all right.'

Rasputin was also in the office, almost unable to contain his impatience. 'What the hell's he doing?'

'Washin' his car.'

'What?'

'I said washin' his car.'

'Look son, if this is your idea of a joke . . .'

'What did he say, Boxer?' Mac's voice was very calm.

'He said to tell you that he'd retired. Hurt. So if you want someone to keep goal don't look to him. He's finished.'

'I'll kill him,' yelled Rasputin. 'I'll flamin' kill him. Who else have we got?'

'Well,' said Mac, getting quickly to his feet. 'I can only think of one person on the staff who used to keep goal, and even in his hey-day he wasn't exactly a Gordon Banks.'

'Who's that?' barked Rasputin.

'Me,' replied Mac quietly.

'So who have they got for a goalie then?' asked Header of his best mate, Jumbo.

'They signed him up from the place we passed on the way from the station,' replied Jumbo.

'Now which place would that be then?'

'The Old Folks' Home. Header. Where else?'

There was loud laughter from the rest of the group that surrounded Header and Jumbo. They were all spoiling for trouble, and they were aware that they were rivals to the Junior Supporters' Club who were standing nearby.

Meanwhile, on the pitch, Mac was nervously shaping up, conscious of his own rustiness and the fact that the match was an important cup tie.

'Come on then, grandad,' shouted Header. 'Let 'em 'ave it.'

'Hit 'em with your pension book,' yelled Jumbo. There were more hoots of laughter from their cronies, and Gerry made as if to move threateningly towards them. But Boxer laid a restraining hand on his arm.

'Take no notice, Gerry. I mean, if you're thick and ignorant it's 'cause you were born thick and ignorant, isn't it?'

Header heard all this, as Boxer knew he would, and he stared at Boxer threateningly. But Boxer gave him a very cool, confident look and Header turned away scowling.

Then there was a roar as a visiting attack surged towards the United goal. Mac tensed, ready for action, and took the shot. He saved it and Boxer and the gang went mad with delight.

'Not bad for an old feller,' yelled Gerry in Header's direction.

Header said nothing and then turned to Jumbo, whispering, 'Did you nick it?'

'Yeah. From the boozer.'

'Show me.'

Jumbo reached into his pocket and furtively brought out a dart. There was another roar of applause from the United supporters as Mac leapt up and punched away a high cross.

Gonk shouted, 'You call 'em strikers. They couldn't strike a match.'

Header scowled again and turned back to Jumbo.

'Go on then.'

'Eh?'

'Let 'im 'ave it.'

'Not me, mate.'

'O.K. Give it to me.'

Jumbo hesitated, and then quickly slipped the dart to Header.

There was another cheer as the United strikers took a goal. Mac was wildly clapping his hands above his head in the goal-mouth below, and there was a tremendous atmosphere of exhilaration and jubilation.

Jumbo said, 'You really gonna do it?'

'Shut up.'

Header took aim at Mac, swung back his hand, and was seen by Boxer as he did so.

'You bastard,' Boxer yelled, jumping on Header. They went down struggling in a scattering section of the crowd, and in a few seconds two policemen were diving after them. A few seconds later, Boxer was dragged out of the crowd and frog-marched from the ground.

'What the hell's goin' on?' asked Gerry.

'I don't know,' said Gonk. 'But I'll tell you this – Boxer's going to be in real trouble.'

'You did all right, mate,' said Rasputin, clapping Mac on the back in the corridor leading to the changing rooms.

'All right?' said Mac. 'Is that all? I was terrific.'

'How do you feel?'

'Knackered.'

Mac stumbled into the changing room, and Rasputin found Cassidy at his elbow.

'It was a good win under the circumstances.'

'What do you mean by that?'

'There was a fight on the terrace.'

'Oh yes?'

'With our people involved.'

'What do you mean, our people?'

'Who else?' replied Cassidy smugly, 'but the Junior Supporters' Club?'

There was a flurried debate about the fight in the club-house after the match.

'You reckon they've taken him down the nick?' asked Gonk.

'Must 'ave,' said Wurzel. 'He'd have been back by now.'

'I can't understand him goin' for that nutter like that. Five minutes before he was holdin' me off,' said Gerry.

'I know somebody who's not gonna be pleased when he hears about it,' said Gonk.

'No prizes for guessing who,' replied Gerry.

'Arrested!'

'Yeah,' said Rasputin. 'And it's that flamin' Junior Supporters' Club of yours again.'

Mac frowned. 'I can't be responsible –'

'The kid *lives* with you, Mac. You *are* responsible.'

Rasputin hurled himself out of the office in a filthy temper, and Mac wearily put his coat on. Katie, who had been typing her way through Rasputin's fury, gave him a sympathetic look. Mac shrugged.

'Those damned kids!' he said.

But just as he was going out, a younger edition of Mac stepped into the office.

'Hi!'

'Andy!'

'How are you, big brother!'

'What the hell are you doing here?'

Andy laughed. 'I had a free day, so I came to watch the match. Didn't expect to see you playing. You did well though. Not bad for an old 'un.'

'Thanks. Hope it taught you a thing or two.'

'So why were you playing?'

'It's a long story. Here – this is Katie, our secretary.'

'Very nice too.'

'O.K. O.K. Here are my home keys.' He passed them across to Andy and then turned to Katie. 'This is my little brother.'

'How sweet,' she replied.

'Look. I've got trouble,' said Mac. 'Go to the house and I'll see you there.'

'Right.'

Andy turned back to Katie. 'I've got plenty to occupy me till you get back,' he said to Mac.

Mac sat in his car outside the police station, with a dishevelled Boxer beside him.

'Look, Mac – if you'll just let me tell you what happened.'

'I don't want to know, son. I know all I need to know. You've been fighting rival fans and you were the one the police charged. *Not* the others.'

'But –'

'Every time a fight breaks out on the ground, it means a hundred fans don't come to watch us any more. Because they're scared to hell it might be them that's involved next time. We've got enough head-bangers and trouble-makers as it is without people who should know better starting fights.'

'Mac. Just listen.'

'No. I don't want to listen.'

Mac slammed the car into gear and drove off. Boxer sat

back in a sulk. Mac had given him no chance to tell his side of the story and seemed determined not to do so. Inwardly Boxer felt empty and afraid.

When they arrived at the house, Mac introduced Boxer to Andy. He was very abrupt, and Boxer was still sulking.

'Boxer – my brother Andy. Boxer's staying with us for a while.'

'How are you?' asked Andy.

'All right,' said Boxer in a barely distinguishable voice.

'Have you had any tea?'

'No,' said Boxer.

'I'll get some chips later.'

'There's a letter for you from Kuwait. His parents are out there,' Mac explained to Andy.

Boxer scanned the letter. 'They're due home next month,' he said.

'Just in time,' replied Mac grimly.

'What –'

'For your first court appearance.'

'Yeah.' Boxer looked away. Then he said abruptly, 'I'm off to the club. See you.'

Boxer went out, very hurt at Mac's continued aggression.

'Bit of a delinquent?' asked Andy.

'He was in a fight on the terrace today.' Mac looked grim.

'Provoked?'

'Somebody's always provoked. It's killing the game.'

Andy was quiet for a moment. 'Katie tells me you've been cooking for yourself while Elaine's away.'

'That's killing me.'

'So how come you turned out today?' asked Andy, desperately changing the subject.

'Our regular goalie's got a broken leg, and the reserve let us down.'

'Making a comeback, are you?'

'No way.'

'But you've got the second leg of the cup tie coming up in a couple of weeks.'

'I know. We're up the creek.'

'I know a goalie who's available.'

'Any good?'

'Not bad.'

'Who is he?'

'Me.'

Mac was silent. Then he said, 'What's wrong with your own club?'

'Itchy feet.'

'You'd be coming down a division.'

'Not for long. Not when I see what United are doing this season.'

'But –'

'And if I stay where I am I'll be down a division anyway. The last couple of matches have been ridiculous.'

'Would they let you go?'

'The manager would be pleased to see the back of me. Seeing as how I've opened my trap a lot about his methods.'

'You'd have to shut it down here.'

'You know what you're talking about. He doesn't.'

'I see.'

'Well?'

'I'll think about it,' said Mac. 'Do you want a cup of tea?'

'He wouldn't even listen!' said Boxer to an eager audience in the club-house that night. 'That's what gets me.'

'Did you tell the police about the dart?' asked Gerry.

'Yeah.'

'What did they say?' asked Gonk.

'They weren't interested. I was just another hooligan to them.'

'Did that nutter throw the dart?' asked the Prof.

'Sure.'

'Then that's the answer.'

'What do you mean?' asked Jenny.

'If he threw it, it must be on the pitch. Somewhere round the goal-mouth. We need to find it. I suggest we organize a search party directly it's light.'

The others looked at the Prof with respect – he always had the ideas. But Boxer was still obsessed by Mac's attitude.

'I mean, I was protecting the guy,' he said.

'Come on, Boxer,' said Gerry. 'You've got to forget this for a bit. Let's play pool.'

'I can't forget it,' said Boxer.

Next morning after a good deal of thought, Mac asked his brother to join the training squad. While Andy was going through the paces, Mac called Rasputin's office and asked him over to have a look at the new player. When he came, Rasputin went overboard.

'He's great,' Rasputin said to Mac.

Mac decided to give his brother a chance, but insisted that because Andy was 'family', Rasputin should take the decision about buying him. While Rasputin went away to think about money, Katie came bouncing up, anxious to know what was happening. As usual, she came straight to the point.

'Do you think he'll buy him?'

'He might,' said Mac.

'He's a funny bloke, isn't he?' said Katie.

'My brother?'

'No, Rasputin.'

'Ah, you've got to know him. He's very canny.'

'And what does canny mean?'

'It's an old Scots expression which is untranslatable,' said Mac with a grin.

*

After a search, the gang found the dart, but not on the pitch. Old Ted had picked it up and was at first loth to part with it. But when he understood the reason why the gang wanted the dart, he gave it to them without a murmur and Wurzel was able to take it to his dad.

Inspector Glossop made a careful examination and then said, 'Did any of the rest of you see this kid throw the dart?'

'No, Dad.'

'Why not? You were all standing next to them?'

'Come on Dad – United had just scored. We were all goin' bananas.'

'I see.'

'But Boxer saw him, which is why he went for him.'

'He says he did.'

'But there's the dart.'

'Could have been planted in the pitch afterwards.'

'He wouldn't do a thing like that.'

'How do you know?'

'Because I know he wouldn't.'

'That's an assurance of his honesty, is it? Being a mate of yours?'

'Why do coppers have such nasty, suspicious minds?'

'Because they spend most of their lives working with suspicious characters. Like you and your mates.'

'So you won't help us then?'

'I'll look into it.'

'When?'

'Down the nick tomorrow.'

Wurzel grinned. 'Thanks, Dad.'

'Don't bank on anything, son.'

'No, Dad.'

But even so, Wurzel felt reassured.

Mac came into the house tired and weary. Rasputin had agreed to take on Andy and he was pleased about that. But the problem with Boxer remained, and Mac was concerned that his parents would be angry that Boxer had run into trouble while living with him. Besides, Boxer was such a nice kid. So Mac was in no mood for Andy, who was anxious to come to Boxer's defence.

'Just a word, Mac,' pleaded Andy.

'No, I'm tired,' said Mac, flinging himself down in a chair.

Just then the bell rang and Boxer, who was in the kitchen, opened the door. He returned with Inspector Glossop.

'Evening, Mac.'

'Hi.'

'Just like a word about the fighting on the terraces the other day.'

'Oh yes?' Mac was instantly wary.

'I thought you might like to know we're not proceeding any further with the case.'

'You're not?' The relief was very evident in Mac's voice.

'No.'

'Why not?'

'I'm sure you've heard Boxer's side of the story.'

Mac looked at him blankly.

'That the only reason he attacked the boy was because he was throwing a dart at you in goal.'

'He was what!' Mac stared at Boxer, who looked away.

'Anyway,' continued Inspector Glossop. 'We've had evidence to substantiate this. So it looks as if our lads grabbed the wrong one. Better luck next time. So that's the end of the matter as far as we're concerned.'

'I'm glad,' said Mac. 'Very glad.'

Boxer showed the inspector out and then returned to face Mac.

'Well – get the kettle on,' said Mac.

'Sure.' He went off to the kitchen.

Andy, doing a passable imitation of John Wayne, said, 'Never apologize, mister. It's a sign of weakness.'

Mac rounded on him. 'I've got news for you. You're in.'

Andy's eyes lit up. 'That's great.'

'So go and get a bath.'

'Why? Queen Mum gonna sign me on?'

'Just the Chairman, and he'll be round in five minutes.'

'Sure, Big Mac.' Andy went out doing a John Wayne walk and Mac threw a book at him. Then Boxer returned with the tea, looking sheepish.

'Thanks,' said Mac. 'For saving my life.'

'Any time, big boy.'

Boxer did a John Wayne walk back into the kitchen this time. With a wild Scots cry, Mac dived after him.

12

Boxer was working out with a bull-worker later that evening when the telephone rang.

'Yeah?'

'Andy Murphy there?' The voice was smooth, confident.

'Who's speaking?'

'Smith. Alec Smith.'

'Hold the line, please.'

Boxer put the phone down and yelled to Andy. 'Telephone.'

'Who is it?' Andy appeared at the top of the stairs in a towel.

'Guy called Smith. Alec Smith.'

Andy's expression changed from a sunny smile to a frown. 'Tell him I'm not in.'

'What?'

'Tell him I'm not in.' His voice was irritable.

Boxer returned to the phone. 'Sorry. He's not in.'

'Oh, thanks.'

''Bye.'

'Goodbye.'

Boxer put down the phone and looked up at Andy. As if struggling for words, Andy said, 'It's this press bloke, see.'

'Oh, yes.'

'He never leaves me alone. Haunts me, he does.'

'Blimey.'

'So if he rings again I'm out. I'm always out. Right?'

'Right.'

Andy went back to the bathroom, and Boxer stood there for a moment, puzzled. Then he shrugged his shoulders and returned to his bull-worker. It was none of his business. Still, it was odd.

'So,' said Boxer to the assembled company of the Junior Supporters' Club in Mac's living room. 'I'll see you all on Thursday night then. I reckon I'll need all the support I can get. That kid's hot stuff.'

'No problem,' said Wurzel. 'You'll murder him.'

'It's all right for you to talk. You won't be in the ring with him.'

Boxer was worried about the fight and he'd been training hard. His opponent was of the same weight and had a good reputation. Boxer knew that he would have to pull out all the stops to beat him. At that moment the bell rang, and Boxer ran to the door.

'Hallo there,' said the stranger.

'Yeah?'

'Andy Murphy in?'

'Who wants him?'

'The name's Smith. Alec Smith. I called the other day.'

'That's right.'

'You gave him my message?'

'Yeah.'

'Is he in?'

'No. He's gone out.'

Instantly Alec Smith assumed a knowing smile. 'You're sure about that?'

'Sure I'm sure.'

'When do you expect him back?'

'Dunno.'

'Oh, well. When he does come back give him this, will you?'

Smith handed Boxer a flat blue envelope with Andy's

name on it. Then he took his leave. Puzzled and wary, Boxer returned to the living room, clutching the envelope rather nervously in his hand. Immediately he arrived, Gonk said, 'I heard that.'

'What do you mean?'

'I heard you say Andy's out, but he went upstairs five minutes ago.'

'I know.'

'So what's goin' on?'

'I'll tell you later. Right?'

'But I –' The sound of footsteps on the stairs reduced Gonk to an uneasy silence. Then Andy came in.

'Andy – that bloke Smith just called,' said Boxer hesitantly.

'Here?' Andy's voice was immediately concerned.

'Yeah.'

'What did you tell him?' asked Andy with sudden unease.

'That you were out.'

'Good lad.'

'He left this for you.'

Boxer handed Andy the envelope and stared at him expectantly. But Andy revealed nothing and walked out of the living room door, expressionlessly. Once upstairs in his bedroom, Andy opened the envelope feverishly. It was full of twenty pound notes. 'Blast,' Andy muttered aloud as he shoved the envelope into a drawer. For a moment he stared at the chest of drawers, as if willing them to burst into flame. Then he flung himself face down on the bed.

Boxer and Becky were playing with a space invader machine in Outer Space when Becky at last managed to blurt out her fears.

'Doesn't it bother you?'

'What?'

'Boxin'.'

'I've been boxin' for years. That's how I got my nickname.'

'But aren't you scared, knowing you're goin' into that ring tonight and that boy'll be hittin' you?'

'A bit nervous. You have to be, else you won't give your best performance.'

'I hate the idea of people thumpin' each other just for sport.'

'Well, it's not as if we're professionals, love.'

'Still –'

'It's all controlled at schoolboy level. You can't get hurt.'

'Mm.'

'So – you're not comin'?' He looked at her anxiously and she grinned back at him.

'I'll come. But I can't promise to enjoy it.'

They stared at each other for a moment, and then Boxer said, 'Blimey. He's in a hurry.'

Derek Cassidy sped past, heading for Rasputin's office.

'Bet that means trouble,' said Becky.

'Guess who I saw Mac talking to on the field just now,' panted Cassidy, his eyes alight with pleasure.

'I'm not a kid,' snapped Rasputin. 'I don't play guessing games.' He was adding up figures again, as usual, and he didn't seem to like the results.

'Mal Madden.'

Rasputin suddenly looked interested – and alarmed.

'Chairman of City?'

'That's right, Mr Jones.'

'What the 'ell's he here for?'

'Social call? Aren't they old friends?'

'Yeah. It was Madden who gave Mac his first break as assistant manager at City.'

'On the other hand . . .' Cassidy smiled. He was going to enjoy this.

'Yeah?'

'City have been having a disastrous run lately.' Cassidy spoke slowly, savouring the effect he was having on Rasputin. 'There *are* rumours they're looking for a new manager.'

'That's right.'

'I suppose . . .'

'You got nothing else to do?' Rasputin's voice was suddenly harsh.

'Of course, Mr Jones,' said Cassidy. 'I just thought you might want to be a jump ahead.'

'Thanks,' said Rasputin, waving a hand in dismissal. 'Now I am.'

'The walls have ears,' said Mac into the phone to Elaine. 'I can't tell you now. But if you can't leave your mother any earlier it'll keep till you come back. O.K. I'll get him.'

Mac put the phone down and went into the living room to fetch Boxer.

'It's the Mother Hen,' he said. 'She wants to blow you a kiss before your fight tonight.'

Twenty minutes later, after Boxer had gone, the phone rang again. Andy sprang to answer it before Mac could move. Once in the hall, Andy closed the door and lifted the phone.

'Hallo.'

'Andy?'

The voice was instantly familiar and Andy put the phone down immediately. He returned to the living room where Mac said, 'Who was that?'

'Wrong number.'

Mac looked at his younger brother quizzically, but Andy had nothing further to say. After an awkward pause, Andy said, 'Well, we off then?'

'Give me five minutes,' said Mac.

As Mac's car pulled away, Alec Smith watched them go.

After a suitable pause, he put his car smoothly into gear and began to follow.

'All right?'

'Yeah.'

The school boxing coach was lacing up Boxer's gloves. The atmosphere in the changing room was tense, and Boxer was very nervous.

They could already hear the mounting tumult in the gym next door, and to Boxer the excited voices sounded like the baying of hungry lions.

'O.K. Off you go.'

Boxer stood up.

'Now remember what I said,' said the coach urgently. 'Don't go mad. Lay off and box him. Right?'

'Right.'

With grim determination Boxer hurried into the gym, where he was met with wild applause from the Junior Supporters' Club. Mac and Andy were also there, clapping enthusiastically.

Wishing that the floor would open and swallow him, Boxer clambered slowly into the ring. Immediately the ref summoned him to meet his opponent, who looked coolly confident. The ref gave them the usual lecture, which was largely drowned by the noise from the spectators.

As the ref continued to instruct the two contestants, Alec Smith walked hurriedly down the corridor outside, guided by the noise. When he arrived at the door he met a young teacher who was selling tickets.

'Do you have a ticket, sir?' he asked politely.

'Haven't had time to get one,' Smith replied smoothly. 'But my lad's appearing tonight. Can I pay?'

'Twenty pence, sir.'

'Cheap at twice the price.'

'Thank you.'

With a switched-on smile, Smith entered the gym, to see

Boxer furiously dancing around the ring, a gang of kids cheering him on and Mac and Andy watching intently. Smith's artificial smile broadened. He wouldn't get away this time – not that boy.

Boxer was getting the worst of the fight as the bell rang for the end of round two, and Andy turned to Mac.

'How many rounds do they have?' he asked.

'Three. One more to go.'

'He must be miles behind on points.'

'You can't win 'em all.'

'He can still win this one.'

Andy suddenly rose to his feet, and watched by Alec Smith, he pushed through the crowd to the ringside.

'Oi.'

'Yeah?'

Boxer looked miserably down at Andy.

'Listen. Use your left jab,' hissed Andy. 'He's wide open to it.'

The coach turned angrily to him. 'Do you mind?'

'I don't mind if you don't mind.'

'I *do* mind. Now buzz off.'

Andy turned to go. 'The left jab, son. That's the one.'

He went back to his seat and the bell rang for the third and final round. Boxer leapt to his feet and went straight into the attack. He also took Andy's advice and began to use a crashing left jab to great advantage, for his opponent immediately went into retreat. Andy leapt to his feet and began to shout, while Mac looked surprised.

Alec Smith scrutinized Andy from his vantage point, and the gang began to yell for Boxer. The fight was over in a few seconds as the ref stepped in to stop the contest, raising Boxer's hand as he did so. Boxer had won, and the coach glanced jealously at Andy. Alec Smith smiled broadly. He knew Andy was a talented lad, and he was a clever lad too. He would soon know what was best for him.

Andy went back to the changing rooms to congratulate a jubilant Boxer. But when he emerged he ran straight into Alec Smith.

'Hallo, Andy.'

'How many times do you have to be told?' His voice was aggressive yet hesitant.

'All I want is a little chat.'

'That's the last thing I want.'

'I think it could be to your advantage.'

'No way.'

'Of course – if you don't *want* to talk to me.'

'I don't.'

'It would be unfortunate if you didn't. Know what I mean?'

Andy scowled. He knew what he meant all right.

It was at that point in the conversation that Boxer was just about to emerge from the changing room. But he recognized Smith's voice and paused to listen.

'I can't see you here,' said Andy. 'My brother's just down the hall.'

'So perhaps you'd like to suggest somewhere.'

'Tomorrow.'

But Alec Smith's expression suddenly hardened. 'No. It's got to be now.'

'All right,' said Andy. 'Follow me.'

Noting the tone of anxiety in Andy's voice, Boxer cautiously waited for a few seconds, came through the door, and began to follow Andy and Alec Smith down the long corridor. They disappeared round a corner and Boxer waited, frozen to the spot. Then he walked a few hesitant paces on until he could hear their voices. What he heard made him far more afraid than he had ever been in the ring.

'A thousand quid. What do you say?' Smith's voice was low and hard.

'No.'

'Two.'

'I say no.'

'You a greedy boy now?'

'How many times do I have to tell you?'

Edging forward, Boxer hit a can that was lying on the floor. He fled through the door of a classroom just as Smith came round the corner.

'What the hell was that?'

He returned to Andy, cursing. 'Could have sworn I heard something. But there's no one there.'

'I've told you once –'

'Look – two thousand for one game. And let's face it, son – it won't be your first time.'

Andy looked at Alec Smith with consuming hatred, and for a moment Smith wondered if he was going to hit him. Then Andy's manner suddenly changed.

'Look – I'll tell you what. You got a telephone number?'

Alec Smith produced a card. 'This is where I'm staying.'

'I'll call you tomorrow.'

'You'd better.'

'I will.'

Andy turned and walked quickly away, back down the corridor. Smith watched him go with a confident smile. Then he strolled off in the opposite direction. Once the corridor was empty, Boxer tiptoed from the classroom door. He had heard every word. But he could hardly believe what he had heard.

13

Later that night, Andy and Mac went out for a meal. They invited Boxer, but he pleaded tiredness and said he wanted to go to bed. Once they had left, however, Boxer went straight into Andy's room and began to search. Somehow he had to ease his mind, somehow he wanted to prove that his suspicions were all some terrible joke, some monstrous misunderstanding. Then, in a drawer, he found the envelope. Cautiously opening it, Boxer found the money. He stood there, shocked, unbelieving. Then, to his horror, he heard the front door opening. Desperately Boxer shoved the money back into the drawer but he knew that he was too late to leave the room.

'Who's that?' Boxer yelled.

Andy's voice came from the bottom of the stairs. 'It's only me. I forgot me wallet.'

He began to ascend the stairs and Boxer shouted desperately, 'It's in the living room, I think.'

'You sure?'

'Yeah – I'm sure.'

'Where are you?' Andy didn't sound convinced.

'I'm in the bath. I was a bit stiff so . . .'

'O.K.'

Andy went into the living room. Upstairs, Boxer hurtled out of Andy's bedroom and dashed into the bathroom. He closed the door gently and leant against it, sweating. Then he heard Andy's voice.

'Found it.'

'Great,' said Boxer.

'See you later.'

'Right.'

Boxer heard the front door slam and he suddenly felt weak at the knees. He sat on the bathroom chair and tried to think. But the shock of his discovery seemed to make his mind totally numb.

After a sleepless night, Boxer went to the club-house and told the gang.

'We've got to tell Mac,' said Jenny when he had finished.

'Tell him what, though?' wondered Boxer.

'About what you 'eard,' said Gonk. 'About the money.'

'We can't really do that,' said the Prof.

'Why not?' asked Wurzel aggressively.

'Well, for starters it's Boxer's word against Andy's, isn't it? Mac's own brother and all that. And we've no proof that he *has* taken a bribe. All we know is that somebody's offered him one.'

'What about the money?' asked Becky.

'So he's got some money in a drawer. So what?' said the Prof.

'Money that Smith gave Boxer to give him,' pointed out Jenny.

But the Prof was adamant. 'Still doesn't prove a thing. I mean, for all we know it could be money owed to Andy. Besides, if we go round accusing Andy of throwing games for money we could be in dead trouble ourselves.'

'What trouble?' asked Wurzel.

'Slander for starters,' continued the Prof. 'You've got to have very solid proof for saying things like that.'

'So what's your suggestion?' asked Wurzel humbly.

'I didn't say I'd got one, did I?'

'So we just sit back,' said Gonk. 'We'll just let him get on with it.'

'All we can do is wait,' replied the Prof calmly. 'Wait and see.'

'You sound like my dad,' said Wurzel crossly.

'Your dad's a cautious man,' said the Prof. 'Like he should be.'

Once Mac had gone out, Andy went up to his room and brought out the money. He thought about it very carefully for a while. Then he went to his wallet, took out a card and went to the telephone. For a moment he hesitated, and then began to dial.

'Yes?'

Andy hesitated again and the voice at the other end repeated, 'Yes?'

'Er – I want to speak to – a Mr Alec Smith,' stuttered Andy.

Mac knew Rasputin was angry directly he came into Mac's office, and he wondered how long it would take him to come to the point.

'Are we going to win today or is it their turn?' he asked.

'They'll give us a game,' replied Mac, still waiting.

'You had a visitor the other day?'

'I have a lot of visitors,' replied Mac cautiously.

'A Mr Mal Madden? Chairman of City?'

'Who told you?'

'A little bird.'

'A little bird named Derek Cassidy? The cuckoo in our nest?'

'Madden just popped in for a chat, did he?'

'He offered me a job.'

'You've got a job, and a two year contract.'

'I told him that.'

'So –'

'It didn't seem to put him off.'

'Why didn't you tell me all this?' Rasputin's voice was openly angry.

'I haven't seen you, have I?'

'What did you tell him?' There was a note of anxiety now in his voice.

'I said I'd think about it. After all – they're half-way up the Second Division – and ambitious.'

'And to hell with us? In mid-season too.'

'That's something else I'll have to think about.'

'I won't release you from that contract. I'll tell you that now.'

Mac paused. Then he said slowly, 'There's something you'd better know, Mr Chairman. I don't know whether I'm staying or going yet. But either way, if I do decide to stay, it won't be because of any threats from you.'

Mac walked out of the office and Rasputin remained there, staring out of the window at the fans coming through the turnstiles. He looked nonplussed.

Mac was playing squash with Andy at the new Sports Centre – and having a hard time of it. Andy was very fit, and the combination of his fitness and his accuracy was very telling. He just had the edge on Mac, and the fact that he was younger also made a difference. Mac, panting and feeling his last hour had come, pounded around the court, sweating and just scraping the ball up from his opponent's fearsome shots.

'Come on, big brother,' yelled Andy, as a point went to him. 'Give us a game then.'

Mac glared at him, stood in the box, and served.

Elaine, who had been urgently summoned home by Mac, was cooking Boxer a marvellous tea – something that he had not had for a considerable length of time.

'All right?' she asked Boxer, who had his head down over a huge plate of bangers and chips.

'Fantastic.' His voice was muffled and dreamy.

'My husband's not exactly the Galloping Gourmet, is he?'

'No comment,' said Boxer.

Elaine moved round the room, tidying and straightening up the devastation that had taken place while she was away.

'Marvellous, isn't it?' she said.

'What is?' asked Boxer.

'I get an urgent call from Mac to come home because he wants to talk to me, and I find he's out playing squash.'

Just then the telephone rang and Elaine rushed out into the hall, hoping the call was from Mac. When she returned, she looked subdued.

'Who was that?' asked Boxer, pushing away his clean plate.

'No one. A man called Smith. He wanted Andy.'

Boxer was immediately on the alert.

'So I told him he was down at the Sports Centre playing squash with Mac.'

Boxer rose to his feet and Elaine looked at him in surprise.

'Where are you going?'

'Out for a while.'

'Funny,' said Elaine. 'I get home and everyone runs for it. You'd think I'd got B.O. or something.'

The squash game was reaching its climax and both Andy and Mac were battling hard to win. Watching them with wry amusement was Rasputin. Andy pressed Mac harder and harder, until he finally hit the winning shot and Mac went sprawling in a desperate attempt to retrieve it. Andy went over to him in concern.

'You O.K.?'

Mac rose painfully to his feet. 'I'm great,' he breathed. 'Just great.'

Above them Rasputin laughed ironically from the gallery.

'It's old age, Mac,' he said. 'It's creeping up on us all.'

'But it hasn't reached you yet, I suppose,' replied Mac.

'Not yet,' said Rasputin.

Andy stayed on the court practising while Mac took a shower. Then the door of the court opened and Boxer popped his head in.

'Want a game?' asked Andy.

'Wouldn't like to show you up,' replied Boxer. 'I've come to warn you.'

'Warn me?'

'That bloke Smith's been after you.'

'Oh.'

'He said you was tryin' to get hold of him.'

'He's lyin' through his teeth.'

'Yeah. See you.'

'Sure.'

Boxer withdrew dejectedly and Andy stood on the court, staring thoughtfully round at the blank walls.

As Boxer emerged from the squash courts, he saw the man briskly leave the car and walk purposefully towards the Sports Centre. Acting on a hunch, Boxer followed him back into the corridor behind the courts. Then the man walked with great precision towards Andy's court and opened the door. Very quickly, Boxer ran lightly up the stairs and hid in the public gallery.

'I got your message,' Smith was saying.

'Yeah.'

'Can we talk?'

'Here's as good as anywhere.'

'Are we on?'

'Sure. It's just this game, right? The second leg of the cup-tie and that's it?'

'You're on.'

'When do I see the money?'

'Half before the game, half when you deliver.'

'Where?'

'When are you next here?'

'I've a court booked for Wednesday at half past seven.'

'I'll see you then.'

Upstairs, Boxer crouched low as he heard Smith make his departure. Then he heard Andy bashing the ball against the wall at a furious pace and he quickly took his leave.

At the club-house, the gang could hardly believe that Andy was being bribed to lose a match. But all the evidence pointed that way, and there also seemed to be depressingly little any of them could do about it.

Gerry told Boxer that he must go to Mac – but Boxer demurred, largely because he felt he had not the slightest shred of real evidence. It was then that the Prof came up with an idea.

'Do you really want to leave United?' asked Elaine.

'Why not?' said Mac. 'It's a good offer.'

This was the reason that Mac had asked Elaine to return home before she was due – the offer that Mal Madden had put to him.

'It's not every day I get asked to manage a team that's still half-way up the Second Division. An ambitious team with money to spend.'

'Well – if it's what you want to do.'

'It's not what *you* want me to do, is it?'

'I never said that.'

'You don't have to.'

'I'm attached to this place,' replied Elaine. 'But it's your career, not mine.'

Mac was silent for a while. Then he said, 'Let me think it over.'

The Prof had hung the microphone of the small, portable tape-recorder over the side of the squash court.

'Won't he notice?' asked Wurzel.

'He's not looking for a mike on a squash court, is he?'

'I dunno,' said Wurzel.

'Look,' snapped Boxer. 'It's our only chance. Now – watch out – he's comin'.'

They all three crouched down in the public gallery and listened to Andy coming on court and beginning to knock up with the ball. Then they heard the door open, and Smith entered. Very cautiously, the Prof switched on the tape-recorder.

'Got it?' asked Andy.

'It's here. I'll see you after the match,' replied Smith.

'O.K.'

They heard the door open, slam, and then the squash ball began to hit the wall again.

'So much for your idea,' hissed Boxer. 'That's no evidence at all.'

Miserably they all crept out, conscious that they had not resolved the situation and unable to think of any way of doing so.

Eventually the gang decided that the only solution was to go to the match and see exactly what Andy did. Old Ted volunteered to drive them, as everyone was too broke, as usual, to afford the fare. So, on the evening of the match, the gang waited on the forecourt of the United ground to see what kind of transport old Ted would produce. He eventually arrived in an extremely battered mini-bus that looked as if it might drop to pieces at any moment. Nevertheless, the doubtful vehicle eventually ferried them to the ground and they stood nervously on the terraces, waiting for the kick-off.

Becky was standing next to Boxer. 'You didn't change your mind about saying something to Mac?'

'No.'

'I wish you had.'

'So do I. Now.'

The game began and Boxer felt his stomach churning with the tension of wondering just what Andy was going to do. Meanwhile, elsewhere in the crowd, Smith was watching. Accompanying him were a couple of heavies who watched Andy with malevolent interest.

A long, looping shot came from the opposition towards the United goal-mouth, and Andy collected it comfortably. Then Boxer let out a howl of dismay as Andy seemed to fumble the ball. It literally slipped through his fingers and, despite a desperate dive, the ball landed in the back of the net. The crowd roared derision and Smith smiled confidently.

At half-time the disconsolate gang gathered together for a drink.

'We've got to contact Mac,' said Gonk. 'He might let in a couple more like that next half.'

Boxer nodded grimly. 'I'm goin' to the dressin' room now – it's our only chance.'

He sprinted off towards the tunnel, but soon found his way blocked by a policeman.

'Where do you think you're going?'

'I've got to see Mac Murphy.'

'Oh yeah?'

'It's important.'

'Goin' to give him some advice about tactics, are you?'

'Look,' said Boxer. 'Don't be stupid.'

'Stupid, am I?' The policeman's mood instantly changed. 'Don't you be so cheeky, son. No one's allowed in there at half-time so buzz off. And if you don't I'll throw you out of the ground.'

Sighing heavily, and knowing he was beaten, Boxer walked slowly back to the gang. There was nothing he could do now. Andy would just have to do his worst.

The play came sweeping back to Andy's goal, and

Smith turned to his heavies with an enthusiastic grin.

'Wait for it, lads,' he said. 'Here comes number two.'

The home striker hit a real blinder towards United's goal-mouth, but to Smith's horror and the gang's amazement, Andy made a very spectacular save. He then spent the rest of the match defending vigorously, and with two minutes to go, faced up to a penalty kick. Once again the home striker hit a real screamer and the ball hurtled past Andy. For a moment, Boxer thought the ball was going in, but Andy pulled off yet another magnificent save. The gang did a war-dance of delight with each other, the crowd went mad, and Smith turned to his heavies with agonized hatred on his face.

'I'll fix him for that,' he said.

Still wild with elation, the kids waited in the car park while Ted struggled unsuccessfully with the recalcitrant engine of the mini-bus.

'I thought you said that thing had gone a hundred thousand miles without a hitch,' said Wurzel.

'Just shut up,' replied Ted.

Meanwhile, Gerry was saying to Boxer, 'Doesn't make sense, does it? I mean, he could have thrown the match easily at least twice if he'd wanted.'

'I know.'

'You're sure you weren't mistaken about the whole thing?'

Boxer shook his head. 'I just couldn't have been. He must have changed his mind, and I can't think why.'

Smith intercepted Andy as he walked out of the club-house.

'I'd like a word with you, chummy.'

'Good. I'd like a word with you. Got something for you.' He proffered Smith the envelope full of money.

'Not here. People might get the wrong idea.'

'So where?'

'Round the back.'

'O.K. Let's get it over with.'

'Just my feelings, too,' said Smith.

'Blimey,' said Becky. 'Just look at that.'

Boxer stared in the direction she was pointing, and saw Andy pinned up against a wall by two heavies. Smith was standing in front of him, waving an envelope. Immediately, Boxer dashed off towards the entrance of the club-house.

'Where are you going?' she yelled.

'To get Mac,' came the faint reply.

'I don't like double-crossers,' said Smith. 'And now you're gonna pay for it. And I can tell you, you won't be playing for a bit when we've finished with you.'

'I told you from the start I didn't want to know,' yelled Andy. 'Last time too. Now you've got your money back, you can call off your gorillas.'

'Not a chance,' snarled Smith. 'I've lost too much money on you, sunshine.'

But just at that moment Mac, Rasputin, Ted, the gang and six burly members of the United team appeared behind him.

'Get your paws off my wee brother,' said Mac, 'or we'll break your necks.'

With instant obedience, the two heavies let go of Andy and beat a swift retreat, closely followed by Smith.

'Friends of yours?' asked Mac.

'I think we just fell out,' replied Andy.

That night, Mac held a party in his living room to which all the team came – as well as the gang. Amid the noisy uproar, Mac demanded an explanation from Andy.

'Look – this guy Smith came up to me last year and wanted to know if I'd like to make some easy money. I'd had a few and I said yes. For a joke.'

'You idiot.'

'O.K. O.K. Anyway, I didn't mean it. But I blew the next match and let in four. Next morning I got this envelope full of money.'

'What did you do with it?' asked Rasputin.

'I gave it back. But I guess he thought I'd got cold feet about taking the money, so he came up with the old routine again.'

'Why didn't you tell me?' yelled Mac angrily. 'I'd have called the police.'

'It doesn't look too good, does it? A player involved in that kind of thing. Mud sticks, Mac.'

'So you decided to teach him a lesson, right?' said Rasputin.

'Right.'

'Mac's right. You *are* an idiot.'

'What would have happened if you'd played a stinker again? I mean, it almost happened, didn't it? Then where'd you be?'

'But I didn't,' said Andy, going to refill his glass. 'I played a blinder and saved the match for you. So it's all right, isn't it?'

He disappeared, grinning, and Rasputin turned to Mac with raised eyebrows.

'Any more at home like him?'

'Just Andy.'

'That's a relief. By the way, I want an answer from you.'

'An answer?'

'You staying or leaving?'

'Well, Mr Chairman, you have me on contract for another two years. And anyway, I wouldn't like to leave a club mid-season.'

'Unless you were sacked.'

'Let's wait and see, shall we?' Mac gave Rasputin a disarming grin and then wandered over to the gang.

'I want to speak to you lot,' he yelled.

'What about?' asked Boxer warily.

'How come you lot knew all about this Andy business? Why didn't you bother to mention it to me? You lot are a real pain in the –'

'Have a crisp,' said Boxer. 'They're cheese and onion.'

In the same series

MURPHY'S MOB
Michael Saunders

Dunmore United is a lousy football club with no future. The team is anchored firmly in the Fourth Division, and the old run-down ground is the haunt of all the local tearaways. When suddenly Mac Murphy takes charge things begin to change – and one of his ideas is to let the kids form their own Supporters Club. Some say it's his worst-ever decision – but Murphy's Mob are determined to prove him right.

BRIAN GLANVILLE'S BOOK OF FOOTBALLERS

Using his incomparable worldwide knowledge of the game, Brian Glanville has compiled an alphabetical guide to great footballers, past and present, European and South American. Many contemporary stars from around the world have been included and every football lover will find it invaluable.

MISCHLING, SECOND DEGREE
Ilse Koehn

Ilse was a 'Mischling', a child of mixed race, a dangerous birthright in Nazi Germany. The perils of an outsider in the Hitler Youth and in girls' military camps make this a vivid and fascinating true story.

TROOPER JACKSON'S STORY

Brian Thompson

It is 1914. War has just started, and Sam Jackson thinks that fighting is glamorous. He will learn.

THE DEVIL ON THE ROAD

Robert Westall

From the award-winning author of *The Machine-Gunners*, a bizarre fantasy about a young motorcyclist who is hurled back in time to the witch-laden seventeenth century.

THE WAVE

Morton Rhue

Nazi-style system sweeps through an American high school when a classroom experiment goes too far. Highlights the dangerous forces of group pressure.

A MIDSUMMER NIGHT'S DEATH

K. M. Peyton

A fast-paced school murder mystery which asks: should you protect your hero-figure at the expense of the truth.